W.i.t.c.h.

Will · Irma · Taranee · Cornelia · Hay Lin

A Choice Is Made

Adapted by ALICE ALFONSI

HYPERION PAPERBACKS FOR CHILDREN
New York

© 2006 Disney Enterprises, Inc.

W.I.T.C.H. Will Irma Taranee Cornelia Hay Lin is a trademark of Disney Enterprises, Inc. Hyperion Paperbacks for Children is an imprint of Disney Children's Book Group, L.L.C.

Printed in the United States of America
First Edition
1 3 5 7 9 10 8 6 4 2

This book is set in 12/16.5 Hiroshige Book.
ISBN 0-7868-4878-2
Visit www.clubwitch.com

I SAY WE SPLIT UP. THEY'RE TOO DANGEROUS IF WE FIGHT THEM ALL TOGETHER.

RIGHT! EACH OF US WILL PICK AN ENEMY TO FIGHT. JUST LIKE THOSE SHOOT-OUTS IN OLD WESTERN MOVIES!

I GET DIBS ON EMBER! FIRE AND WATER DON'T MIX.

I'VE GOT A SCORE TO SETTLE WITH KHOR!

GOOD! THAT LEAVES THE REST OF US WITH NERISSA . . .

NO!

GOOD THINKING, IRMA! IN THAT CASE, I'LL TAKE TRIDART.

CALEB, I NEED YOU TO HELP CORNELIA TAKE ON SHAGON.

YOU GOT IT, WILL! I'VE SEEN WHAT HE'S LIKE,* AND I KNOW HOW DANGEROUS HE IS.

WILL! ARE YOU GOING TO BATTLE NERISSA ALL BY YOURSELF?

NO, I WON'T BE ALONE. I'LL HAVE THE STAR OF CASSIDY BY MY SIDE.

THE STAR IS THE ONLY THING THAT CAN HELP ME HOLD OUT AGAINST THE POWER OF THE HEART OF CANDRACAR.

*See W.i.t.c.h. #17.

ONE

Omigosh, Hay Lin thought, fluttering her wings, *what* is happening?

She tried to fly but couldn't. The Star of Cassidy had formed a transparent cube surrounding her, the other Guardians, and Cornelia's boyfriend, Caleb.

The Oracle called this invisible cage an "ethereal shield." But Hay Lin didn't care what the clear-box prison was called. She felt like a helpless doll in a plastic package. And she did *not* want to be sealed up like that! Not with her grandmother out in the open and Nerissa about to strike!

Pressing her nose against the shield's clear wall, Hay Lin looked at her grandmother below. Wearing a robe of radiant white, the old woman strolled across the Temple's ornate floor. She appeared totally at ease.

"Unbelievable," Hay Lin whispered to herself.

Her grandmother didn't seem at all scared or worried. When she reached the center of the vast hall, she calmly sat cross-legged in the meditation circle with the Oracle and the other Elders of the Congregation.

Hay Lin wasn't feeling nearly so tranquil. She frantically searched out Nerissa. The evil crone was at the other end of the hall, raising her staff and shutting her eyes. Hay Lin held her breath, waiting for her to attack.

But Nerissa didn't attack—at least not in the way Hay Lin had expected. She didn't conjure up bolts of energy. She didn't shout or threaten or display any of her typical vile behavior. Instead, she simply murmured the words of a spell.

When Will had carried the Heart of Candracar, radiant light had always shone from its center. But under Nerissa's spell, the dazzling pendant turned blacker than an eclipse.

Then the Heart cracked!

Hay Lin gasped. Like dark blood from a

gaping wound, thick black fluid flowed from the Heart of Candracar and rained down inside the Temple. The liquid pooled on the jeweled floor. It stained the ornate walls and endless stairways. It tarred the intricately carved crystal columns.

As the repulsive muck blighted the Temple structure, Hay Lin looked at the other Guardians sealed up in the shield with her. Irma and Taranee appeared confused. Will seemed angry, and Cornelia looked totally frustrated. Hay Lin felt all of those emotions, too, especially the frustration.

"We were ready to fight fireballs, lightning, almost anything that sorcerer could dish," Hay Lin murmured to herself. "But not *this*. How do we fight *this*?"

A sea of darkness was swiftly blotting out the pure, shining light of the Temple. Beauty and good were being suffocated under a flood of ugliness and evil.

But if evil blots out Candracar, what will happen to the other worlds? Hay Lin wondered. Will chaos break out? Will every world be darkened by violence and hatred?

The possibilities were terrifying.

Her grandmother had once told the Guardians that Candracar had been created eons before, when the universe had split in two. After that, there had been two separate factions: those who wanted peace and those who lived on the pain of others. "Living on the pain of others is exactly what Nerissa is doing now," Hay Lin whispered. "All that hateful hag wants is revenge!"

And Hay Lin knew why.

Long ago, the sorceress had been the Keeper of the Heart, just like Will. But her lust for the Heart's power had led her to betray her duty and kill her fellow Guardian Cassidy.

The Oracle and the Elders of the Congregation had been outraged. They had punished Nerissa by imprisoning her inside a mountain tomb. For this, Nerissa never forgave them. And when she escaped her prison, she vowed to take revenge on the Oracle and all of Candracar.

Never in Hay Lin's darkest dreams had she thought that Candracar could be attacked, let alone destroyed. Yet at this very moment, its destruction seemed inevitable, and she couldn't do a thing about it!

Across the hall, Nerissa, in her scarlet gown,

tossed her hair over her shoulder. Then she began to laugh. She and her deadly assistants hadn't been touched by the foul black tar. They were sealed inside their own ethereal shield, safe from the filth now choking the majestic Temple.

Hay Lin and her friends were also safe, inside the Star of Cassidy. But the Oracle and the Elders of the Congregation were in grave danger. While they sat in their meditation circle, index fingers touching, lips moving in a silent chant, a black cloud moved over their heads. Hay Lin knew they didn't have much time.

"That blob thing is reaching the Oracle and the Elders!" Irma cried, her hands pressing against the shield.

"Oh, no!" Hay Lin shouted. "Grandma! Get out of there! Run!"

But her grandmother didn't run. She just kept sitting there, with the dark flood rising around her.

"Omigosh!" Cornelia cried. "That black liquid is swallowing them up!"

"No-o-o!" Hay Lin couldn't understand why her grandmother and the others didn't try to escape.

Suddenly, Will's eyes opened wide. "I hear the Oracle's voice," she whispered. "He's telling me to abide . . . by the decisions . . . of the Heart."

Hay Lin was barely listening. She was feeling desperate now. Her grandmother was very dear to her. Hay Lin loved her parents, of course, but since the time when she'd been very little they'd been busy 24-7 running the family restaurant. And it was her grandmother who'd told her Chinese legends at bedtime. It was her grandmother who had dried her tears and always made time for her. It was her grandmother who had revealed to Hay Lin and her friends their true destinies. . . .

Hay Lin well remembered that day. She and her friends had gathered in her family's kitchen for tea and cookies—and to share their bizarre stories. Each of them had been experiencing strange new abilities to manipulate water, fire, earth, and air. And all of them had had dreams about a dazzling crystal medallion. That was when Hay Lin's grandmother had entered the kitchen, holding the mysterious Heart of Candracar.

"You are the new Guardians," she had said to them, *"the most important warriors in a battle that was started thousands of years ago. The forces of nature lie within you . . . now and forever, they will be with you.*

"You, Irma, will have the power over water— broken and uncontainable. To you, firm Cornelia, the power of earth. To you, generous Taranee—the difficult gift of fire. And you, my little Hay Lin: you will be free and light as air."

The last girl to hear of her destiny was Will, designated as the Keeper of the Heart. She would be the Guardian who carried the Heart of Candracar, the magic orb that was the key to the Guardians' powers. It strengthened and united the girls, making them invincible.

Because Will was charged with carrying the Heart and keeping it safe, she would become the leader of W.I.T.C.H.—the name the girls had given their group by combining their first initials.

At first, Will had been hesitant about the whole leadership thing. But with the help of her friends, she had embraced her destiny. She'd become strong and courageous in her role.

Eventually, however, the responsibility of

carrying the Heart had worn Will down. One night, she'd completely lost control. In a moment of weakness, Will had been tricked by Nerissa into handing over the Heart.

That was the reason the evil sorceress had been able to penetrate Candracar's formidable defenses. Once the Heart was in Nerissa's possession, even the Elders had been stunned by her strength.

Hay Lin had been hoping that the Star of Cassidy would be strong enough to defeat Nerissa. After all, Hay Lin thought, we went to an awful lot of trouble to find it in the first place!

"But what good is it doing us now?" she murmured to herself. The Star was supposed to help the Guardians protect Candracar, not seal them all up like plastic toys, unable to fight back!

Just then, Hay Lin noticed that some of the black streams from the cracked Heart were beginning to bend and curl unnaturally. Like grasping fingers, they reached out toward the Guardians.

Alarmed, Caleb stepped in front of Cornelia. "The negative essence of the Heart of Candracar!" he cried. "Evil in its purest form—

and now it wants us, too!"

"But it can't get through the ethereal shield," Will assured them all. "In here, we're safe."

We're safe, Hay Lin thought. But my grandmother isn't. "Grandma!" she cried.

Relentlessly the dark rain poured, and the pool of evil rose. Hay Lin's grandmother never looked up. The old woman simply remained cross-legged in the meditation circle, chanting with the Oracle and the Elders as the thick tar closed over their heads.

"No-o-o-o!" Hay Lin shouted.

Her grandmother's death in Heatherfield had been the cruelest thing Hay Lin had ever experienced. It had felt as though she'd lost a part of herself. But not long afterward, Hay Lin had begun to hear her grandmother's voice inside her head.

Was it a distant memory of her words? Hay Lin had wondered at the time. Or was her grandmother actually speaking from another place?

Back then, Hay Lin hadn't known the answer. But when the Guardians finally traveled to Candracar, she had understood.

Candracar was where her grandmother had gone after her death on earth. There, W.I.T.C.H. had finally met the Oracle—the all-seeing, all-knowing being who watched over all the worlds of the universe. Hay Lin had been reunited with her grandmother, and when that happened, Hay Lin's broken heart had healed.

"I lost my grandma once," Hay Lin whispered to herself. "I *can't* lose her again!"

The Oracle had warned the Guardians not to try to harm the ethereal shield. But Hay Lin couldn't just stand there and watch her grandmother be obliterated by evil!

With both fists, she battered the invisible wall in front of her. But it did no good. The rubbery surface gave a little, but it refused to break. Feeling helpless beyond words, Hay Lin began to cry.

It's hopeless, she thought, sinking to her knees. What do I do?

From somewhere deep inside, Hay Lin heard her grandmother's voice: *Do not be afraid, my little Hay Lin. No matter what happens, I will always be a part of you. . . .*

Tears slipping down her cheeks, Hay Lin turned toward her friends. Taranee put an arm around her, and both of them looked to Will for guidance. But the Keeper didn't look right all of a sudden. She put a hand to her head as if something were affecting her.

Then, for some unknown reason, a strange sleepiness appeared to overwhelm Will . . . and she slowly closed her eyes.

TWO

Will opened her eyes.

Light, she thought. *Bright light.*

Just a moment before, darkness had been closing in on her, but now . . .

Will blinked. She was lying down. The glaring rays of the dawning sun poured in through a window. She turned her head away from the dazzling brilliance and found herself face to face with . . . her stuffed green frog?!

"What the . . .?"

Will sat up, eyes wide, heart beating in double time. What was her favorite stuffed animal doing in Candracar?

She shook her head, looked around, and realized that she was no longer in another dimension.

Neither was she inside an ethereal shield or a vast, timeless temple. She was sitting in her very own bedroom, on her very own froggy bed-sheets, wearing her favorite froggy pajamas. Her fuzzy frog slippers were right there on the floor beside her bed, where she always left them.

"What happened to Candracar?" she murmured, scratching her head under her sleep-mussed red hair. "How can I be back in my room?"

Outside the window the day looked beautiful. The early morning sun was shining. Birds were singing, and—

Chomp!

"Ouch!" Will cried.

Her pet dormouse had just jumped onto the bed and introduced her hand to his needlelike teeth.

"Okay, dormouse," Will told the furry little creature, "if you wanted to prove this wasn't a dream, you've done it."

The dormouse scampered over to her stuffed frog and began to nibble on its leg. With a sigh, Will pulled the squirrel-like animal away from the stuffed toy.

"Hey, take it easy!" she told the dormouse. "I'll get you something to eat."

As Will grabbed the box of crunchy pet food from her bookshelf, she ran her hand along the surface of her desk. It felt solid enough.

Can I really be home? she wondered. Or is this just an illusion?

Will flexed a muscle and pinched her arm. She felt wide awake. But something was definitely missing. She held up her open palm and called on the incredible, burning energy that lived inside her—

But there was nothing there.

"There's one thing I'm sure of," she whispered. "I don't feel the presence of the Star of Cassidy anymore."

Her insides felt different now. To any other girl, any *regular* girl, everything would have felt just fine . . . totally normal. But Will wasn't a regular girl. She vividly remembered what it had felt like to carry the dazzling brilliance of Cassidy's Star. With it gone, Will felt cold and hollow.

Will frowned, realizing that this was exactly how she'd felt after Nerissa had tricked her into giving up the Heart of Candracar. The heavy feeling of responsibility was gone, but so was that incredible power, that profound, intense magic.

Will's shoulders slumped, and she sank back down onto her bed. Now that the radiant energy was no longer burning inside her, she felt a little lost.

"Hey, there, kiddo!" Will's mother suddenly swung open the bedroom door. "Don't tell me you're up already!"

Will blinked. Another shock, she thought. The sun had just risen. It was obviously really early, and yet her mother was already dressed for work!

Will's mom's business suit was completely wrinkle free, and her makeup and hair looked totally perfect. Plus, she was grinning from ear to ear—and Will's mother was *not* a morning person. *Stand back! I'm late for work!* would have been perfect wording for a bumper sticker for her car.

"Mom?" Will asked, rubbing her eyes. "Is that really you?"

Will's mother laughed. "I was wrong," she said. "You're obviously still sleeping!"

Will shook her head and covered her face

with a pillow. Whoa, she thought, This is just *too* weird!

"Go ahead, and keep your eyes shut," her mother teased. "But use your nose to find your way into the kitchen!"

Will did. After she fed her dormouse, she cleaned up, got dressed, and found her mom again, at the kitchen counter. A plate of fresh-baked croissants sat in front of Mrs. Vandom. She was pouring two steaming mugs of tea.

"I've got a pretty good chance of getting to work *almost on* time today," her mom told her.

Will took a sip of tea. It was . . . delicious! But how? Will wondered. Her mother's tea usually came in two flavors—weak as dishwater or strong enough to choke on. This morning, however, her ratio of tea to water was pretty close to perfect.

Cautiously, Will reached for a croissant. They were a beautiful golden brown. But appearances could be very deceiving where her mother's cooking was concerned. So she wasn't letting her guard down. Will still remembered the time her mom had served some delicious-looking roast beef to Will and some guests. After slicing through the perfectly browned meat, they'd found the insides still frozen solid.

With a deep, shaky breath, Will took a small bite of the golden croissant. She chewed and swallowed, then shook her head in complete disbelief.

If pastry could take you to heaven, she was on a cloud with a harp. The dough was perfect, outside and in—tender and flaky and so buttery it practically melted on her tongue.

This can't be right, she thought.

Will took two more bites just to make sure, then another sip of the tea. It was all absolutely amazing!

A few minutes later, Will's mother was smiling and waving as she headed out the kitchen door. "Off to work. Have a good day, kiddo!"

Will nodded, lifting her half-eaten croissant in a salute and wondering what was going on. Her mom had waked her on time and with a smile. They'd shared a scrumptious, homemade breakfast. And they hadn't fought *once*.

The whole thing might have made Will happy—if she'd been remotely used to that kind of normality. But Will's life hadn't been "normal" for a very long time.

I *know* I'm not dreaming, she thought,

shaking her head. I can smell my tea, taste my croissant, feel my clothes. But something's *off* here. Way, *way* off.

An hour later Will caught up to her fellow Guardians on the front lawn of the Sheffield Institute. Irma, Taranee, Cornelia, and Hay Lin were hanging out beneath a tall oak. As the majestic tree dipped its long branches in the brisk breeze, wayward leaves spiraled around the girls' makeshift circle.

Will told her friends about her truly bizarre morning, including waking up without the Star of Cassidy. Nobody seemed surprised. In fact, all of the Guardians told her that they were experiencing the very same loss.

"No more powers?" Will asked her best friends in disbelief.

"Nope," Hay Lin and Taranee said.

"*Nada,*" Irma replied.

"Not a trace," Cornelia agreed.

Irma shrugged. "I can't even make a drop of water dance around."

"Same thing with fire," Taranee added, pushing up her large, round glasses. "I can't control it anymore."

Cornelia nodded, her long blond hair lifting with the leaves on the strong breeze. "It looks like the power of earth has left me."

"And my powers over air seem to have flown the coop!" Hay Lin exclaimed, flapping her arms, then giving a little laugh.

Will scratched her head. Every one of the Guardians had lost her powers during the same night. Yet nobody seemed all that upset. Hay Lin was practically making a joke of it.

"No big deal," said Irma. "I mean, we've already seen our powers drop to minimum levels."

Irma was right, and Will knew it. Twice before, the Guardians had found themselves without the ability to magnify their elemental abilities.

The first time, it had happened after they'd defeated Prince Phobos on the world of Meridian. W.I.T.C.H. had been united and strong during that difficult struggle. But after it was over . . . Will sighed, remembering how badly things had gone. The Guardians had begun to bicker and pick silly fights with one another. And as their friendship had begun to break down, so had their powers.

They had noticed it because of a few little things: Irma had transformed herself into her mature Guardian form to impress Andrew Hornby, but then not been able to transform back into her normal self; Taranee had lost her ability to communicate telepathically; and Hay Lin's power over air had been totally deflated.

Then Will's mom had announced that she'd gotten a job transfer to another city. By the end of the year, she and Will were supposed to be moving out of Heatherfield. Will had pitched a fit. Her mother had forced her to move once already. The last thing Will wanted to do was move again.

She and her best friends had worried that that would be the end of W.I.T.C.H. Which was why Will had agreed to use the power of the Heart in a way that wasn't exactly legit.

Irma, Hay Lin, and Will had gone to the offices where Will's mother worked. Their plan was simple: destroy her mom's transfer papers, and Will wouldn't have to move!

They had sneaked into the human resources department. And when Hay Lin's power over air failed, they had decided to call on the Heart to help them break open the company safe.

But things had not gone according to plan. An Elder in Candracar named Luba had been working against them all along. The moment they'd misused the Heart, she'd sabotaged them from Candracar.

The Power of Five started to weaken. Though the girls still felt in their hearts that they had their Guardian powers, they were in fact not as powerful as they once had been. And, for the first time, the girls were unable to use those powers. They had to learn to come back together as a group to regain the full extent of their powers.

The loss of their powers had happened again more recently. Will had been feeling stressed out by the heavy responsibilities of the Heart. And Nerissa had made things worse by constantly invading Will's dreams and turning them into nightmares.

Will was tired, confused, and more than a little frustrated. Because of Nerissa's tricks, she had begun to believe that her best friends were out to get her. And one night, during a big school party, she'd turned on them.

Instead of fighting Will, however, the other Guardians had simply stood firm. Finally, Will had come to her senses. She had realized that Nerissa had tricked her. Her friends were still her friends after all.

But Will had felt so ashamed about her behavior that she'd made herself a target again. She shuddered now, remembering how she'd run to see Matt Olsen that night.

After messing up so badly, she'd desperately wanted Matt to make her feel better. She'd wanted his affection and understanding. And she'd so wanted him finally to say, "I accept everything about you," that she'd confided all her secrets to him—about being the Keeper, about Candracar, and about the Heart.

Unfortunately, Matt hadn't been able to give her any comfort that night, because it wasn't really Matt she'd been talking to! Nerissa had taken over his body. So when "Matt" had asked Will if he could hold the Heart, Will had given it freely to him. She'd never suspected that she was handing Nerissa the power to destroy Candracar.

It's because of me Nerissa has the Heart now, Will thought, mentally kicking herself for the hundredth time since that night.

The Heart was what magnified and united the Guardians. So it made perfect sense that without its energy, the girls of W.I.T.C.H. would only possess their minimum abilities.

Luckily, it hadn't been long before Will had located the Star of Cassidy. With the Star in Will's possession, the Guardians' powers were fully restored once more.

But as Will sat with her friends on the Sheffield lawn, something still didn't make sense to her. Even if she didn't have the Heart of Candracar or the Star of Cassidy, the Guardians should have retained some ability to manipulate earth, fire, water, and air.

"This time it seems we've lost our powers completely," Will pointed out to the other Guardians. And, of course, without their powers, there was no way to get back to Candracar and defend it.

With a sigh, Will leaned back against the trunk of the big oak tree. She hugged her knees, trying to puzzle out what was happening and what to do about it. But she didn't have a clue.

"What worries me the most about all of

this," she told her best friends, "is that none of us seems to be very upset about it." Instead of being angry or worried, everyone appeared to be almost . . . *happier.* "It's as though a weight's been lifted from our shoulders."

"Girls!" shouted a familiar voice. "The school bell has long since rung!"

Will and the others looked up to find the school principal marching toward them. Mrs. Knickerbocker was a matronly woman with a large bosom, big glasses, and a gray beehive hairdo. She wore dark blue suits and mannish red ties and had all the charm of a prison warden.

"Um, thanks, Mrs. Knickerbocker," Will replied, rising from under the tree. "I guess we didn't hear it."

"Well, I guess you'll have to get moving, then!" bellowed the principal. "Now, march!"

The girls walked toward the school entrance. Irma turned her head and rolled her eyes so that only her friends could see. Taranee and Hay Lin put hands over their mouths to stifle their giggles.

Behind them, Mrs. Knickerbocker struck a severe pose as she planted her two plump fists on her substantial hips. "You think I enjoy being a guardian?" she called after them.

This time Taranee rolled her eyes. "I'd say so," she whispered.

Irma giggled. "I bet she eats dog biscuits for breakfast."

Will and Cornelia were the only ones not joining in the gibes as the girls strode toward homeroom. Things were really bad in Candracar. The Star of Cassidy was gone, and the Guardians had lost every trace of their powers.

Despite all that, Hay Lin, Irma, and Taranee were all *laughing*.

I don't get it, thought Will. It's like they've already forgotten how serious the situation is!

THREE

Brrrinnngg!

Every day, it's always the same, thought Taranee. One minute, my classmates are ready to nod off at their desks. And the next, they're Olympic sprinters, racing each other to get to the front door. Those energy-drink companies would make millions if they could just find a way to bottle Sheffield's final bell!

"Hey, Taranee!" called Hay Lin. She was standing in the crowded hallway. "Over here!"

Taranee pushed up her round glasses and made her way over to her friend. As one of the top students at Sheffield, Taranee was always lugging home a heavy load of library books—along with a heavy feeling of worry as to whether she was studying enough to keep up her straight-A record.

Today, however, Taranee felt differently. . . .

I'm sick of doing homework, she thought. I want to do something fun! Maybe Hay Lin will invite us over to the Silver Dragon. Or maybe Cornelia will know about some funky new boutique we can check out downtown.

Taranee caught up with Hay Lin, and together they headed for the front doors. On the way, they fell into step beside Irma, Cornelia, and Will.

Irma looked almost as happy as Hay Lin about the end of the school day. But Will and Cornelia looked as though they were still working out equations in Mr. Horseberg's math class.

What's with them? Taranee wondered. After all, it's a beautiful day, and we're *free*!

But Will obviously didn't get that. With a superserious expression, she turned to the other Guardians. "So," she said, "should we go back to where we left off talking?"

Taranee scratched her head in confusion. *Talking?* she thought.

"Talking about what?" Hay Lin asked.

Will's jaw dropped. "Our powers, Hay Lin!"

she replied. "We've got to decide what to do!"

"Yeah, yeah, right," Hay Lin replied with a dismissive wave of her hand. "Could we talk about it later on?"

Will stared at Hay Lin as if she'd just received a slap in the face. But Hay Lin didn't seem to notice.

Frankly, Taranee couldn't see why Will was trying to bring them all down. What was wrong with taking a break? Couldn't they forget their troubles for one afternoon?

By then the girls had reached the front courtyard of the school. Hay Lin pointed to a lanky boy with short black hair. He was leaning next to a stone column, finishing up a call on his cell phone.

"There's Eric!" Hay Lin squealed.

Eric Lyndon had lived all over the world. He'd recently moved to Heatherfield, and now he was living and studying at the Heatherfield Observatory with his grandfather, astronomy professor Zachary Lyndon.

"I'm going over to say hi," Hay Lin announced to her friends. "Then I'll be back, okay?"

Taranee wasn't surprised. Hay Lin had been

crushin' on Eric since the two had met the previous summer. They'd been dating on and off ever since.

"Hey, there!" Hay Lin said as she walked up to Eric.

Taranee and the other Guardians inched a little closer to the pair, to eavesdrop.

"Why the long face?" Hay Lin asked.

"Hi," Eric replied. "I just got a call from my grandfather. Some delinquent broke into the observatory and wrecked the entire planetarium!"

Uh-oh, thought Taranee.

Her memory was kind of fuzzy, but Taranee definitely knew who was responsible for all that vandalism—the Guardians!

It had all started when Eric and his grandfather had claimed they had located the coordinates for the Star of Cassidy. They told the Guardians about it, but they'd also claimed that there was nothing in the sky to see. The Star was supposed to be there, but it wasn't.

Will had wanted to see for herself, so she sweet-talked the Guardians into breaking in to the observatory with her. Then, she sweet-talked the alarm system into staying quiet.

Once they were inside, Will had gone straight to the observatory's huge telescope. The coordinates had already been set for Cassidy's Star. But when Taranee and the other Guardians looked through the viewfinder, they didn't see anything—just a plain old night sky.

When Will looked through the telescope, however, she saw the most amazing, dazzling light in the universe! The next thing Taranee knew, Will was talking to thin air. But it wasn't really thin air. Later, Will told the Guardians that Cassidy's spirit had descended from the heavens to speak to her. After Nerissa had stolen the Heart of Candracar, Cassidy's spirit had wanted to help the Guardians. So she delivered her own resplendent energy to Will.

Unfortunately, before Will could call upon the Star of Cassidy to restore W.I.T.C.H.'s powers, Nerissa had sent her henchman, Khor, to destroy them all. The fight had been positively nasty at first; the girls' powers had been weak. With a vicious roar, Khor had begun throwing the girls around. They had held him off, but he had started to score some painful bull's-eyes.

Finally, Will had used the Star to transform and reunite the girls. Back in full-power mode, the Guardians struck back. Khor was soon yelping and running away in fear. The whole battle had been totally fantastic.

Now Taranee held her breath as she listened to Eric talk about the wrecked planetarium. Hay Lin looked a little nervous and guilty.

Uh-oh, Taranee thought again. Is she going to spill, and tell Eric what really happened?

Hay Lin cleared her throat. "Well, Eric . . . if you . . . uh, need a hand cleaning up, I'm free this afternoon!"

Eric shrugged. "Why not? Thanks."

Taranee smiled with relief. Thank goodness Hay Lin kept our secret, she thought. But when she turned to Will and Cornelia, they were grimacing.

"Something funny is going on here," Will said quietly. "It's not like Hay Lin to act this way."

"Yeah," Cornelia agreed. "In Candracar, she was devastated when she saw her grandma trapped in that black goo. But now it's like she's not even thinking about it. It's as if she's blotted it out completely. . . ."

"I don't understand her, either!" Irma piped up. Will and Cornelia turned toward Irma, who then exclaimed, "This school has guys who are way cuter than Eric!"

Taranee laughed as Irma linked arms with her. "For example," Irma continued conspiratorially, "ever seen *him*?"

She pointed to two guys walking across the school lawn. The first was "Joke Man" Mason. He was skinny and wore glasses and was always cracking bad jokes.

Taranee knew Irma wasn't crushin' on Joke Man. The guy she was talking about had broad shoulders and longish blond surfer-dude hair. He had a really hot smile, wore a thumb ring, and spent most of his time hanging out with the supercool extreme-sports guys.

Taranee nodded as the two boys walked right by. "I've seen him," she whispered to Irma. "He's a new kid. He just moved to town, and he's in his last year of school."

"Well, he *just* smiled at me," said Irma, giving her hair an *I'm all that* toss.

Taranee rolled her eyes. "Um, Irma . . . that was a grimace of pain. Joke Man just elbowed Mr. Hottie in the ribs."

"But he *did* look my way," Irma pointed out.

Taranee tapped her chin. "You know, I think

you're right. He does keep glancing over at you."

Irma grinned. And Taranee frowned.

With Hay Lin and Irma crushin' on guys, Taranee couldn't help wishing she could be with her boyfriend, too. She searched the lawn until she found him—Nigel. There he stood, wearing baggy jeans and a distressed jacket. He had shy brown eyes that sparkled when he laughed and the kindest, sweetest smile she'd ever known.

In Taranee's opinion, he was far cuter *and* cooler than any of the other Guardians' boyfriends. But Taranee's mother, Judge Cook, didn't agree.

Taranee had gone on a wonderfully romantic date with Nigel. They had shared more than a few meaningful looks. But then her mother had forbidden her to see him. Why? Because, as a judge, she'd personally sentenced him to community service for breaking into the Heatherfield Museum.

Man, Taranee thought, if my mom could have seen me breaking and entering at the Heatherfield Observatory last night . . . !

The only reason Nigel had gone to the

museum in the first place was a dare. Back then, the Guardians had been fighting evil in Metamoor. A portal had opened inside the museum, and the snake-man, Cedric, had come through it to the earth.

A rumor had spread throughout Heatherfield that there was a monster in the museum. And that was why Nigel had agreed to sneak in with Uriah and his gang of troublemakers. They'd wanted to see the so-called monster. Then the alarm had been tripped, and security arrested them.

So, okay, Nigel *had* been a member of Uriah's delinquent skateboarding crew. The gang of Outfielders did things like tangle the handlebars of bicycles together at the school bike rack and throw stink bombs into the restrooms.

Nigel had always been a reluctant member of Uriah's gang. Most of the time, he was the one who tried to talk the group out of doing anything really destructive or dangerous.

Taranee thought her mother had been totally unfair to Nigel. He wasn't like Uriah and his lowlife pals. Nigel was different. He was cool and kind and considerate.

When Judge Cook laid down the law about Nigel, Taranee had tried to argue. But her mother argued for a *living*, so it was nearly impossible to get her to change her mind.

Then Taranee's life had grown complicated. Her teachers began piling on the homework. And she and her friends went through some major stress when Nerissa arrived on the scene. For weeks now, Guardian business had kept Taranee crazy busy—and kept Nigel out of her life.

But today, for some reason, Taranee didn't feel very stressed. In fact, her heavy worries about everything from her grades to her Guardian powers seemed temporarily to have vanished. She felt lighthearted. She felt carefree. She felt ready to do something radical!

Seeing Nigel on the school lawn, the breeze tousling his chin-length brown hair, had made Taranee forget many things. She forgot about being a good daughter, a good student, even a good Guardian.

She also forgot about being shy!

I just can't help myself, Taranee thought, walking right up to Nigel on the lawn. Nigel is so cool and sweet. I've got to let him know how

I really feel about our relationship!

"Hi, Nigel!" Taranee said. "I've been thinking about you a lot lately."

"Really?" he replied.

Taranee held her breath for a second—until a welcoming smile broke over his handsome face.

"Me, too," he admitted softly. "I mean, I've actually n*ever sto*pped thinking about you."

Taranee smiled and enjoyed sharing a romantic moment with her crush, Nigel. The day was turning out to be a pretty good day after all.

FOUR

Will's eyes had practically bugged out as she watched Taranee walk over to Nigel. It was the last thing she expected to see happen.

"Come on, Cornelia, how can you tell me any of this is normal?" Will cried.

First Hay Lin had blown them off to help Eric. Then Irma had left to follow some blond hottie she'd been crushin' on. And now Taranee was jumping ship!

"It's not normal, Will," Cornelia assured her. "Something strange is going on. Look at Taranee. She just saw Nigel, and she's lost it!"

Will shook her head, wondering what to do next. Each of the

37

Guardians, except for her and Cornelia, seemed to have forgotten about Candracar.

"Things are *so* not right it's scary," Will whispered.

They had to figure out what was happening to them, solve the problem, and get back to Candracar to stop Nerissa. But how were they going to do that when *three* out of their Power of Five didn't even care that they'd *completely* lost their powers? They had no ability to make the wind change direction, to bend streams of water, or to cause blazing fires to appear.

Just then, Will noticed an attractive woman striding across the school grounds. Her face was a severe triangle, her black hair blunt-cut to her pointy chin. And her long, lean silhouette looked even longer and leaner in a perfectly tailored plum-colored business suit.

"Uh-oh. Trouble's coming," Will warned Cornelia. "Taranee's mother just showed up."

"*What?* Where?" Cornelia cried.

Will pointed out Judge Cook.

The woman's expression looked superserious as she scanned the crowded lawn. Then again, Will thought, when *doesn't* the woman look superserious? Mrs. Cook was a judge, after all. And, according to Taranee, the woman judged things 24-7!

Cornelia grabbed Will's arm. "She's forbidden Taranee to see Nigel," she rasped. "We've got to do something."

"Do something?" Will replied. "Like what?"

"We have to distract her," Cornelia insisted, pulling Will across the grass. "If she catches them, there'll be trouble!"

Will was a little afraid of Judge Cook. So she wasn't all that jazzed about Cornelia's idea. But before she could protest or come up with a better plan, Cornelia had dragged her right up to Taranee's mother.

"Hello, Mrs. Cook! Are you looking for Taranee?" Cornelia chirped.

For a moment, Judge Cook seemed a bit distracted. Her gaze continued to roam over the crowd of kids. After a few seconds, however, she looked down at Cornelia and Will.

"I had to pick her up today," she told them. Her expression remained sober. She didn't even try to return Cornelia's fake smile. "Have you seen her anywhere in this mad crowd?"

"Actually, she's already gone," Cornelia lied, crossing her fingers behind her back.

Mrs. Cook stared intently at Cornelia, who glanced at Will for support. Will knew what Cornelia wanted her to do. But she wasn't at all comfortable fibbing to a judge. That is, until Cornelia jammed her elbow into Will's side—*hard*.

"Isn't that *right*, Will?" Cornelia prompted.

"Ow!" cried Will. "Um . . . I mean . . . yep!"

Will cleared her throat and tried to fake a grin as wide as Cornelia's. It wasn't easy. Cornelia had been an Infielder for years. She'd always been popular and part of the in groups at school. So, of course, she'd had plenty of practice in faking her emotions and shining people on.

Will had always been a bit of a rogue. She prided herself on always having a firm sense of her own identity. She was forever wearing slouchy jeans, hoodies, and scuffed-up basketball shoes. Her mop of red hair was usually partly hanging in her eyes and in need of a trim. A tomboy through and through, Will just didn't care about dressing like the masses.

Cornelia was just the opposite. She was seldom seen without the trendiest designer skirt or cashmere sweater on her slender frame. Her long, superstraight blond hair was so sleek it looked as if she'd just stepped out of a spa. And she put a high priority on always looking her best.

Despite their differences, however, Will really respected Cornelia, who had courageously risked her life to fight evil and keep her fellow Guardians safe. And after everything Cornelia had gone through in loving and almost losing Caleb, Will found her to be the most mature of their group.

Whether Will was agonizing over Matt, suffering under the weight of the Heart, or fighting with her mother, Cornelia seemed to understand what Will was going through better than any other members of W.I.T.C.H. did. Despite their friction in the past, Will realized that Cornelia had become a really close friend.

Will didn't want to let Cornelia down, or Taranee, for that matter. So, even though Will was really bad at lying to people, she did her level best to fake a smile for Mrs. Cook.

"She's out with Irma," Will told Taranee's mother through gritted teeth, "who knows where?"

For a few seconds, Judge Cook studied Will

and Cornelia. Then she raised a dark eyebrow.

"Girls," the judge said sternly, "do you know what I do for a living?"

Will gulped. "You're . . . you're a judge?"

"Exactly." Mrs. Cook folded her arms and narrowed her eyes. "And I can assure you that I have a real knack for smelling lies."

"But we're not liars!" Cornelia protested.

"Of course not," Mrs. Cook replied. "You're *good friends*, which in this case is even worse! Now, if you'll excuse me—"

"But, Mrs. Cook—" Cornelia called out.

It was too late, Will realized. Mrs. Cook had already taken a few steps, before stopping frozen in her tracks. The woman was now looking straight at her daughter, who was *holding hands* with a boy she herself had sentenced to community service for breaking and entering.

"Taranee!" shouted Mrs. Cook.

Taranee looked up. Her happy face instantly fell. So did Nigel's. In fact, as he stood next to Taranee, Nigel looked like a wild animal caught in the crosshairs of a hunter's scope.

Oh, man, Will wailed to herself as Mrs. Cook marched over to her daughter. This is gonna be brutal.

Despite Will's frustration with Taranee, her heart went out to her friend. Nigel might have hung out with a posse of jerk-faced creeps, but he was far from being one himself.

Will remembered that time he'd come to her rescue. She had still been the new girl at Sheffield, having just moved to Heatherfield from Fadden Hills, and she felt awkward and a little unsure of herself.

Uriah, the pimply-faced, spiky-haired leader of a small gang of troublemakers, had already picked on her once. And then, Will had come across him in Heatherfield Park while biking home from school.

Uriah was trying to trap an innocent little dormouse. The other thugs in his gang stood by, watching. There was hulking Laurent, with the buzz cut and donkey laugh. And there was short, potbellied Kurt, with the perpetual smirk. Nigel was there, too, but he had been trying to talk Uriah out of his plan.

Uriah had thought it would be funny to catch the dormouse and throw it into geeky Martin Tubbs's locker. But the dormouse just wasn't going for that. He bit Uriah hard on the finger and scampered away.

Uriah was furious at the animal. He picked up a stick and went after the little critter. If he couldn't catch the dormouse then he would smash him!

That was when Will ran up and got between Uriah and the dormouse. She'd yelled at Uriah to back off. The dormouse had been saved, but Will had given Uriah a whole new target—herself.

Uriah started closing in, but then Nigel stepped between Will and Uriah and placed a firm hand on the bully's shoulder. Uriah backed down, and the gang of creeps left her alone.

Well, not *totally* alone, Will recalled.

She'd made friends with the dormouse, who later became her pet. And she'd met a guy who'd been nice enough to come over and help her with the animal—Matt Olsen. *He* later became her boyfriend.

In the end, Nigel had turned out to be a really good person. He quit Uriah's gang. He really liked Taranee. He was really sweet about expressing his feelings, too.

One day, when Taranee had had to take

photographs of insects for biology, he'd left her a box with her name on it. Inside was a beautiful butterfly.

Will knew how Taranee felt about Nigel. He was the kind of guy she just wasn't going to give up easily. On the other hand, she didn't look all that confident about holding his hand when Judge Cook marched over to her!

"Mom, I . . ." Taranee began to explain, but her voice trailed off in a choked whisper.

"We're late," Judge Cook snapped, planting her hands on her hips, "and I still have a lot of errands to run."

Taranee swallowed hard, silently staring at her mother.

The judge's dark gaze left her daughter's face and settled on the nervous-looking boy still holding Taranee's hand.

"Hello, Nigel," the judge said with complete calm. "You don't mind if Taranee and I dash off, do you?"

Nigel blinked. He appeared as stunned as Taranee. It took him a few seconds to find his voice. "Um, of course not, Mrs. Cook," he finally said.

Mrs. Cook nodded and took Taranee's arm. As they turned and walked toward the street, Will and Cornelia hurried up behind them to hear their exchange.

"I don't understand," Taranee told her mother. "Aren't you mad at me?"

Mrs. Cook stopped walking and faced her daughter. "Last night I had a long talk with your father," she said. Her serious expression seemed to soften a bit. "He convinced me to give the young man a second chance."

The news *sounded* good, but Taranee's tense face failed to relax. And Will knew why. Taranee had once told the Guardians that she could never read her mother. Whenever Judge Cook softened her expression, it usually meant she was deep in thought, searching for the perfect way to win their arguments. So it was no surprise to Will that Taranee wasn't willing to trust her own ears.

"What . . . what do you *mean*?" Taranee cautiously asked her mom. She held her breath waiting for the reply.

"I mean . . . tonight we're going to rent a movie and order a pizza," Mrs. Cook said. A smile finally came over her face. "Do you want to invite him?" she asked, cocking her head toward Nigel.

Taranee's jaw dropped. Then her eyes widened, and her face beamed brighter than the afternoon sun.

"Are you kidding?" she cried.

Her mother laughed. "That is, if you feel like spending the evening with two old fogies—"

Mrs. Cook hadn't finished talking, but Taranee was through listening. She was already running back to her boyfriend.

"Nigel! Nigel!" she squealed.

When she reached him, she threw her arms around his neck. Then she *kissed* him. Right on the lips! Right in front of her mother and everyone!

"Nigel! Oh, Nigel," Taranee gushed with a blissful sigh.

Whoa! Will thought. What happened to the shy, bookish Taranee?

She glanced at Cornelia. But she didn't appear to have any answers. In fact, Cornelia looked just about as stunned as Will felt.

I don't know what's going on here, thought Will. But there's one thing I do know. This *weird* day just got *weirder*!

FIVE

"Guess it's just you and me," Cornelia said to Will with a shrug.

Will nodded, and the two girls left the school grounds. Neither had ridden their bikes to school that morning, and Cornelia was suddenly feeling really wiped out. She wasn't looking forward to a long walk home.

As they reached the sidewalk outside the school, Cornelia noticed a city bus just pulling up to the stop.

Swishhhhhhh!

"Do you want to take the bus with me?" Cornelia asked.

"Sure," replied Will.

The girls ran a half block to reach the bus before it pulled away. They climbed aboard, paid their fares, and worked their way through the crowded aisle. Every seat was taken at that hour. So they gave up trying to find one and simply stood together near the back door.

With a rumble, the motor started up, and the bus took off in a cloud of exhaust fumes. Cornelia lunged for one of the hanging straps to keep from losing her balance. Will took hold of a nearby metal pole.

For a few minutes, they remained silent and just gazed absently out the windows, watching the sights of Heatherfield roll by.

There were soaring skyscrapers and squat wooden newsstands; block-long department stores and tiny boutiques; old stone residential buildings and brand-new restaurants. And parading through it all was traffic, traffic, traffic. Trucks, cars, and motorbikes clogged every side street and intersection.

Some of Cornelia's relatives lived in the suburbs. They said they didn't like Heatherfield— or any big city. They didn't like all the noise and commotion, all the chaos. But Cornelia loved it. She loved the lights and the commerce. She loved looking at people of all shapes and sizes, all creeds and colors, all rushing off to get things done in their busy lives.

Everything seemed very alive in the city, especially at that hour. The streets virtually pulsed with dynamic energy. To Cornelia, it wasn't intimidating or irritating. It was reassuring.

She loved Heatherfield. She loved its people. Protecting them—and all the worlds of the universe—from evil was an important job. She was proud to be a Guardian; she couldn't believe that Hay Lin, Irma, and Taranee could blow the job off so easily.

After five long minutes of staring absentmindedly at the bustling city outside, Cornelia turned to Will and asked, "So what do you think we should do?"

"I don't know," Will said, looking genuinely perplexed. "I just don't get what happened back at school. It's not normal."

"No," Cornelia agreed. "It's definitely not normal."

All of a sudden, Will's confused expression turned guilty. "I mean, I'm happy for Taranee and everything," she said firmly. "But . . ."

"I understand you perfectly, Will," Cornelia

replied, nodding her head with a sigh.

"You do?"

Cornelia nodded. "It's as if the others were taking everything too lightly."

Will nodded in agreement, and Cornelia sighed. Just like Will, she wanted Taranee to be happy. She wanted every member of W.I.T.C.H. to be happy. But not at the expense of their responsibilities as Guardians—and especially not when Candracar needed their help so desperately.

Just then, Cornelia noticed a row of familiar residential buildings outside the window. That was Will's block. Cornelia was standing right next to the *stop* buzzer. She reached up and rang it, for Will.

"Maybe we've all just gotten the lives we deserve," said Will. "Ever think of that?"

"You mean . . . a life without powers?" asked Cornelia.

"A life without *problems*," Will clarified. "But maybe . . . maybe they're the same exact thing."

As the bus came to a stop, Cornelia shuddered. She wondered how Will could even *think* that. Had she already forgotten what Hay

Lin's grandmother had told them all? Magic was their destiny. Without it, they would be only half alive.

"Cornelia!" Will cried.

"What?" Cornelia shouted, alarmed by Will's tone.

"Duh!" Will threw up her arms, gesturing at the neighborhood around them. "Why did you get off, too? This is my stop."

"Oh!" Cornelia realized that she'd been so wrapped up in their conversation she'd climbed off the bus right behind Will. She quickly spun around to get back on the bus, but it was already rumbling away.

Buh-bye! she thought, feeling her cheeks burn with embarrassment. Wow, did I flake out, or what?

Cornelia threw Will a sheepish smile. "What was I thinking?" Then she shrugged. "Guess I'll just wait for the next bus. If you have to go, there's no problem."

Will laughed. "Are you kidding? You're not going to wait by yourself. I'll wait with you. We have lots to talk about."

Cornelia sighed with relief. She was glad Will had decided to wait with her. The weather was turning colder, and she didn't want to be alone.

She drew her coat more tightly around her body as they talked. But neither she nor Will could come up with a solution to their problem.

I should be able to think of something, Cornelia thought. After all, I've been able to come up with pretty good suggestions for W.I.T.C.H. in the past.

When Nerissa kept invading the Guardians' dreams and turning them into nightmares, the girls had nearly gone crazy from lack of sleep. Cornelia had suggested that they all come over to her place for a pajama party. If they were all sleeping in the same place, she reasoned, their dreams could join together and they could fight the evil sorceress as a team.

The girls had agreed to try it. And it had actually worked. Okay, so they hadn't been able to destroy Nerissa totally. But at least they'd gotten her out of their dream lives for a while!

Why can't I come up with something as clever as that this time? Cornelia asked herself. But nothing brilliant was coming to mind. She glanced over at Will, but she'd fallen silent, too.

So the two girls just stood there thinking in the cold.

"Wait a second," Cornelia whispered.

"What?" asked Will.

"It's not like W.I.T.C.H. hasn't been in tough situations before," Cornelia pointed out.

"True," Will agreed.

If Cornelia had learned anything in the last year, it was this: the most important thing about being a part of W.I.T.C.H. was sticking together. Whenever the Guardians bickered and fought, whenever they doubted each other or tried to go their own ways, they had failed. But when they stuck together—for example, uniting in their dreams to defeat Nerissa's nightmares—they had done just fine.

"You know what I say?" Cornelia exclaimed, suddenly energized. "Let's get everyone together later this afternoon, at my house!"

That's it, she thought. If we all just get together and puzzle this out as a team, we'll be sure to figure out what's going on and find a solution.

Will nodded excitedly, strands of her red hair falling into her eyes. "Sure thing!" she agreed, pushing the unruly hair back. "We've got to try to snap the others out of—"

Brrrinnngg-brrrinngg! Brrrinngg-brrrinngg!

The sound of a bicycle bell had distracted Will. Cornelia looked up to see Matt Olsen slowing his bike to a stop near the curb.

"Am I interrupting something?" he asked.

"Matt?" said Will, clearly surprised to see him.

Cornelia was surprised, too. Matt and Will had endured a lot of misunderstandings over the last few months. Things had been pretty uneasy between them.

"Hi!" Matt said, flashing Will his thousand-watt smile. "I was hoping I'd run into you. I went to your apartment. But nobody answered at your place."

"You . . . you were waiting for me?" asked Will.

Cornelia furrowed her brow. She didn't like the strange look that had come over Will's face all of a sudden. One second, the girl was totally fired up about solving their problems. And the next, her features were a complete blank.

Matt rubbed his strong jaw, which was

covered with just the right amount of stubble to make him look both rugged and cool. "I just wanted to ask if you felt like helping me out at my grandpa's pet show this afternoon," he said.

"Are you kidding?" cried Will. A huge grin broke over her previously blank face. "I totally feel like it!"

"Cool!" Matt replied, grinning back. He slapped the flat area behind the bicycle seat. "Hop on, and I'll give you a ride."

"Do you mind, Cornelia? I mean, the bus should be here any minute, and we already talked about everything, didn't we?" Will asked.

Cornelia noticed that Will didn't even bother waiting for an answer. She was already climbing onto the bike and taking hold of Matt's solid shoulders.

Cornelia had barely put her hand up in a wave good-bye before Will turned around to face front. Then Matt's muscular legs began to spin the bike pedals, and they took off from the sidewalk.

For a stunned minute, Cornelia watched Matt's bike speed down the busy street. Will's bright pink backpack grew smaller and smaller as the two rocketed away. Then they turned the corner and were gone.

I can't believe it, Cornelia thought, letting out an exasperated sigh. And they all say *I'm* the love-struck one!

She shook her head and began to pace nervously up and down the sidewalk. She felt totally alone now. Will had been the only one who sensed that something wasn't right. But seeing Matt was all it took to make her forget about their current predicament.

It's so bizarre, Cornelia thought. When Matt asked Will to go with him, she'd used the exact same words as Taranee had when her mom had said it was okay to see Nigel.

"Are you kidding?" they had both said.

"And I wish they were," Cornelia whispered. "I wish they *all* were!"

It was as if Will and Taranee had forgotten about their roles, their mission. Hay Lin and Irma were no better. The air Guardian had completely forgotten her best friends once she'd met up with Eric. And then there was the way Irma had gone off after that boy she didn't even know . . .

Arrrrgh! Cornelia clenched her fists just

thinking about how many times the water Guardian had left her steamed. And today was no exception!

On the other hand, she thought as she continued to pace the sidewalk, Will's never looked happier.

Cornelia tried to consider this seriously.

Maybe our powers *are* too much responsibility, she thought. Seeing Matt again had really transformed Will. One second she was worried and confused, troubled by dozens of questions. And the next, she suddenly forgot about the questions and was totally carefree. She seemed genuinely happy.

For a long time now, Nerissa had been unrelenting in her assaults. And being the Keeper made Will the worst target of all. That evil woman had made Will a nervous wreck.

Cornelia couldn't recall the last time she'd seen Will as happy as she'd been on the back of Matt's bicycle. So . . . could Will have been right when she'd said, "Maybe we've all just gotten the lives we deserve"?

Was a life without powers also a life without problems? Was it really that simple?

I know one thing for sure, Cornelia thought.

There's a very good reason I don't ever want to give up the responsibility of being a Guardian—Caleb. I don't want to forget him. No matter what problems we might be going through. I've already forgotten him once, and that's *never* going to happen again!

Cornelia closed her eyes and conjured up the image of the boy she loved, the boy she'd dreamed about even before she'd met him. In her mind she could still see the young warrior with his sad green eyes, powerful body, and even more powerful determination. She recalled the first time they'd met in the city of Meridian, in his world of Metamoor. It seemed like so long ago.

She'd gone through a portal—an invisible tunnel from Heatherfield to Caleb's world—and ended up nearly drowning in an impossibly deep fountain on the other side.

Cornelia had traveled alone on that trip to Metamoor, without the other Guardians to help her. She could easily have drowned. But Caleb had rescued her. He'd jumped into the deep water and fished her out.

"You're safe now. . . ." his deep voice had reassured her.

Cornelia remembered how his strong arms had carried her away from that Gothic fountain in the palace. She remembered how stunned she'd been to look up and see him. She'd slowly reached out and stroked his cheek, just to make sure he was real. She'd studied his smooth skin and piercing green eyes, immediately sensing the warmth and courage in his spirit. It was an instant connection, intense and genuine.

Is it really him? she'd wondered. *Is this really the boy from my dreams?*

Even before she knew Caleb's name, Cornelia had been dreaming of him. She knew his face so well that she'd been able to describe every one of his features to her best friend, Elyon. One day, Elyon had surprised Cornelia by presenting her with a picture of her dream boy—and when she saw him in person for the first time, she'd recognized him instantly.

Cornelia sighed. She vividly remembered all of those times from her past—not only the day she'd met Caleb, but all of the tender moments she'd shared with him since.

For some reason, she just couldn't recall when she'd *last* seen him.

"Okay, so I don't know where he is right now," she murmured to herself, "but I just can't forget him. I can't. . . ."

Just then, Cornelia heard the approaching rumble of a large motor. The next city bus was about to pass her stop. She quickly waved her arm to make sure the driver saw her.

Swishhhhhhh!

The bus pulled up to the curb. But as Cornelia waited for the door to open, a movement in the corner of her eye distracted her.

Cheep-cheep! Cheep-cheep!

Cornelia looked up to see a blackbird perched on a street sign right over her head. He was squawking like mad.

Cheep-cheep! Cheep-cheep!

"What the—?!" Cornelia blinked in surprise. The blackbird was staring down right at her as it sang.

Cheep-cheep! Cheep-cheep!

"Wait a minute . . . I know this bird," she whispered. The old Guardian Kadma had had a blackbird just like that.

The bird lingered on its perch a moment longer, then flapped its shiny dark wings and flew into the air. Cornelia watched it circle overhead like a small black kite; she had a strong feeling that it was waiting for her to follow.

It must be Kadma's bird, Cheepee! Cornelia decided. And if it is Cheepee, he can't be here by pure coincidence.

She waved to the bus driver to go ahead. He closed the doors and pulled away without her. Then she followed Cheepee down the street.

There was no doubt the bird was leading her. He would fly for a while, then stop and perch on a sign or a tree branch until Cornelia caught up. Once she did, he'd take off again.

Cheep-cheep! Cheep-cheep!

"I'm coming, I'm coming!" she called.

This is definitely not normal, Cornelia thought. And that thought just confirmed her suspicions that there was something peculiar causing the Guardians to act so strangely.

"Yeah," she whispered, "there must be a spell or something like that behind all this."

If the bird were leading her to Kadma, then maybe she'd be able to help, reasoned Cornelia. After all, Kadma had served as a Guardian along with Nerissa and Cassidy. With all of her years of experience, maybe she would be able to figure out what was happening to Will and the others.

As the blackbird continued to lead Cornelia up one street and down another, she felt her spirits rise in hope. Once, Cornelia had been uncomfortable with the idea of having special powers. And, for a long time, she'd been the most skeptical member of W.I.T.C.H.

But not today.

Today, Cornelia found herself wanting to believe in magic more desperately than ever.

SIX

In the small, green park across from the Heatherfield train station, Kadma paced back and forth. Where *is* that bird, she fretted silently. How long could it take to find that little redheaded Keeper?

Kadma stopped pacing and fumbled with her silk shawl, adjusting it around her long, high-necked gown. Although Kadma was very old, she looked a fraction of her age. Her dark brown, almond-shaped eyes were still bright and alert. Her flawless skin had few wrinkles. And the threads of silver in her long black braid only added a regal air to her overall elegant appearance.

But there was nothing regal or composed about her internal turmoil. "This day started out badly, and it's only getting worse!" she grumbled, plopping down on a park bench.

A short time before, she'd arrived by train from Fadden Hills. When she reached the street, she'd sent Cheepee off to find Will Vandom.

Kadma didn't like coming to Heatherfield, but after what had happened that morning, she had nowhere else to turn. She could only hope that the Keeper of the Heart of Candracar would have some answers.

But where is that bird of mine? Kadma wondered. Hasn't he located Will yet?

Cheep-cheep! Cheep-cheep!

Hearing her blackbird's familiar call, Kadma quickly rose from the bench. She looked up, shading her eyes from the strong afternoon light. A few moments later, she caught sight of the bird across the busy street. He was circling low in the air, in front of the train station's big clock. The slanting golden rays of sun were reflected off his ink-black feathers.

Thank goodness, thought Kadma, sighing with relief.

She was about to call out telepathically to

Cheepee. But then she remembered. . . . She couldn't. Even the smallest traces of her powers were gone. They had vanished that very morning.

"Cheepee!" She called out to the bird the old-fashioned way—with her voice.

Cheep-cheep! Cheep-cheep!

The blackbird swooped down, right to her. Kadma lifted her arm, and he lightly perched on the back of her hand.

Just then, a pretty blond girl ran up to her. She wore a long, checkered wool skirt, red suede boots, and a soft gray jacket, and she carried a magenta backpack. She looked out of breath.

"You're . . . Kadma . . . I hope!" the girl said, huffing and puffing.

It took a moment for Kadma to recognize the stranger. Something about her seemed familiar. "Cornelia?" she said. "Why, of course. Cheepee must have sensed that you and I were connected in some way. . . . But my bird knows perfectly well that I don't wish to speak with *you*," she snapped. "Good-bye!"

"Hey, hold on!" Cornelia cried.

Kadma ignored the girl. At that moment, she

wasn't interested in talking to anybody but Will. So she crisply turned away from the little blond Guardian and began to walk further into the park.

But Cornelia turned out to be as stubborn an earth Guardian as Kadma was. A simple good-bye wasn't enough to get rid of her.

"I'm sorry I disappointed you," Cornelia said, blocking Kadma's path, "but I have no intention of letting you leave."

Well, Kadma thought, this girl obviously has no idea who she is dealing with! The old Guardian straightened her posture and looked down her narrow nose at Cornelia's determined pout.

"If you think you're going to stop me," she warned, in a voice of cold steel, "you're sadly mistaken."

Kadma was about to storm off in the other direction when Cheepee surprised her. Without permission, he flew off her hand and up to the tree limb just above them.

"Cheepee!" Kadma called in surprise.

But the bird wouldn't move. It appeared as though he wanted to force Kadma into staying there and talking things over with Cornelia.

Kadma was far from happy about this. She was an imperious woman who liked to be in complete control of her surroundings. That was one reason she seldom left her large estate in Fadden Hills. Being forced into any situation made her feel uneasy.

She turned to Cornelia and scowled. "I used to have the same powers as you," she said, narrowing her eyes at the young Guardian, "those of the earth."

"Exactly!" Cornelia replied, putting up her hands. "You used to. Now we're even."

"What do you mean?" asked Kadma.

"Just what I said!" Cornelia exclaimed. Then her angry posture appeared to wilt into one of resignation. "I don't have magical powers anymore, either."

Kadma's dark eyes widened in shock. Her fury dissolved as quickly as Cornelia's, and she suddenly felt deflated, too.

"May the stars help us," she said. "I have to . . . I have to sit down." She noticed a fountain a few steps away. It had a large base and a wide concrete ledge.

"What's going on?" Cornelia asked as Kadma sank down on to the hard stone. "Do you know anything about it?"

"I barely know why I'm here in this city," Kadma admitted, shaking her head. "I never leave my estate."

"You mean the Rising Star Foundation in Fadden Hills?" Cornelia pressed.

"Yes!" Kadma replied, putting a hand up to her throbbing head.

Oh, blast, she thought. I hate being reminded of the past. That's why I didn't want to see anyone but Will. She already knows this story, this piece of ancient history I want only to forget!

But Kadma couldn't forget. Once, she had been proud of being a Guardian, just like Cornelia. But then . . . she rubbed her aching forehead. What a fool she'd been! She'd loved her duties, loved her friends. She'd thought of her life as a beautiful picture, painted in eternal colors. She had never thought that that picture could be altered.

But she'd been wrong. Her life hadn't been a picture at all. It had been a puzzle—and a fragile one. And a few unfortunate events had broken it into a thousand unrecognizable pieces.

At that time, Nerissa had been the Keeper of the Heart. She had been good once, strong and brave. She had been proud of her duty as Keeper. But that pride had soured into vanity. She had turned down a very dark path.

She began to care only for the Heart's power, neglecting the duty with which it came. Her fellow Guardians had tried to set her right, but she turned on them.

One day, the Oracle took the Heart away from Nerissa. He entrusted it to her fellow Guardian, Cassidy. But that wasn't the end of the story.

Kadma's eyes glistened with tears at the memory of what came next.

Blinded by jealousy, Nerissa had lured Cassidy into a trap and killed her. Too late to save Cassidy, Kadma and the other Guardians had captured Nerissa and taken her to Candracar. There, she had stood trial for Cassidy's murder.

After the Oracle and the Elders of the Congregation sentenced Nerissa, Kadma and Halinor together rose up and angrily confronted the Oracle. They were in terrible pain over the loss of their friend Cassidy, and they just couldn't see why it had had to happen.

They blamed the Oracle for his part in the events. They said he must have known what would happen to Cassidy, but that he had given her the Heart all the same.

The Oracle refused to respond to their charges. Instead, he retired Kadma and Halinor as Guardians and banned them from Candracar.

Because they had questioned the Oracle's authority, Kadma and Halinor would never join Yan Lin as Elders in Candracar. They would remain outcasts.

Kadma and Halinor returned to the earth and moved into a large mansion in Fadden Hills. There they established the Rising Star Foundation, an organization that helped children without homes and families. But the organization was something else, too. It was an earthly memorial to their fellow Guardian, the brave, sweet Keeper named Cassidy.

Knowing that Will Vandom would be the next Keeper, Halinor had decided to watch over her. Using disciples from Rising Star, she had kept a close eye on Will as she grew up.

Will never suspected, of course, that her

teacher, babysitter, swim coach, and others in her life were all spying on her. They were reporting back to Halinor about her progress.

Halinor had passed away before Will had ever met her. But she had left her a diary with some very important information—the coordinates for finding Cassidy's Star.

Kadma knew that the Star of Cassidy would help Will and the other Guardians fight Nerissa. But when she had risen that morning and felt cold emptiness inside her, she had feared the worst. Had something happened to Will? Had the Star been damaged?

Kadma turned to Cornelia. "The point is," she told the girl, "something a little strange happened, and I wanted to talk about it with Will in person."

"What happened?" Cornelia whispered, her blue eyes looking worried. "Tell me. . . . Please."

"Even when we go into retirement, we Guardians keep a trace of our powers," Kadma explained. "It's a sort of magic touch that never leaves us. We call it an Eternal Gift."

She raised her eyes to Cheepee, perched nearby on the tree limb. For years now, she'd been able to communicate with her bird through her thoughts. As of this morning, however, she seemed not to be able to talk to him any longer. It made her feel sad and lonely, the way she'd felt when Halinor had passed away.

Nevertheless, thought Kadma, telepathy or not, Cheepee is still a loyal and well-trained companion. She raised her arm and he obediently flew down. Once again, he perched lightly on the back of her hand. She gave him a small smile.

"A trace of your powers?" Cornelia repeated. "What do you mean?"

"Earth was my element," Kadma replied. "So, for instance, I kept my remarkably green thumb." That was why a greenhouse, containing a glorious winter garden, had been attached to one wing of the Rising Star Foundation mansion. No matter what time of year it was, the greenhouse was always filled with lush vegetation and blooming flowers.

"Since my retirement, my power has been quite weak compared to what it once was," she said. "But it had always been there . . . until this morning. When I woke up, it had vanished entirely."

Cornelia gasped. "Just like what happened to me and the other Guardians!"

Kadma shook her head, seeing the distress on Cornelia's face. "Destiny is a strange thing," she told the girl. "This might not be such a bad thing, after all. What for you is a problem, for me is a liberation. . . ."

"Liberation?" Cornelia asked. "How?"

Kadma smiled down at Cheepee, still perched on her hand. Suddenly, she lifted it, launching the blackbird into the air, giving him the freedom to stretch his wings.

Cornelia's bright gaze followed the bird. She watched him fly high in the air, so high that she had to shade her eyes to see where he was going.

"Now there's nothing that connects me to Candracar any longer," Kadma told Cornelia.

The young Guardian quickly brought her gaze back to earth. Her eyes met Kadma's. "First the girls forget everything, and now you!"

Kadma furrowed her brow. "Forget?"

"Yes!" Cornelia exclaimed in frustration. "They're acting like this stuff about our powers doesn't matter to them. Like they—"

"They had *never* felt magical, you mean?"

Kadma asked, suddenly very serious.

Cornelia nodded.

Kadma's jaw went slack. "That's it, then," she whispered. "I didn't believe it could ever have happened, but there's no other explanation."

"What are you talking about?" Cornelia asked.

Kadma rose from her seat. When she'd lost her powers that morning, she had imagined a dozen scenarios. She thought, for example, that perhaps the Oracle had decided to pull the plug on her personally, taking away the last remnants of even her smallest powers.

But when she heard what Cornelia had to say about the Guardians' *forgetting*, she knew what was happening. There was only one possible explanation. And it was much more serious than Kadma had ever thought.

How do I get this through to Cornelia? she thought. How do I make the girl realize what's happening?

Stepping closer, Kadma reached out and placed two shaking hands on the young Guardian's shoulders.

"Don't you understand, Cornelia?" she said,

her voice soft but urgent. "It's all so incredibly clear. . . . Candracar *no longer exists!*"

Cornelia stared at Kadma. Her eyes were wide and her mind full of questions. How could this be? What would become of the Oracle and the Council of Elders? And what about Caleb? The news was hard to comprehend. She had to gather the others and tell them—fast.

SEVEN

"I hope this doesn't take too long," said Taranee, checking her wristwatch. "Nigel's coming over tonight."

"Wait!" said Hay Lin. "Am I hearing right? Did you say, *Nigel*?"

"Yeah, hold the phone!" said Irma. She turned to Taranee. "Since when did you become a rebel? Didn't your mom lay down the law about seeing him again?"

"Yes," Taranee replied, "but—"

"*Hey!* I made a joke!" Irma interrupted, suddenly remembering what Taranee's mother did for a living. "Get it? Lay down the *law*."

Taranee rolled her eyes. "We get it."

"Okay, so the joke was semi-lame," Irma admitted. "So *sue* me!"

Hay Lin and Will groaned.

"Okay, I'll stop," Irma promised. "So what's the four-one-one on your mother's reversal of attitude? Or are you just seeing Nigel on the sly?"

Taranee took a sip of her milk shake. "Well, it all happened just after school. My mom showed up and saw me holding hands with Nigel, and—"

"What?" interrupted Hay Lin. "Judge Cook showed up at school? And she saw you and Nigel together? You're kidding! How did I miss that?"

"You went off with Eric," Will reminded her.

"Oh, yeah!" said Hay Lin. "And I'm seeing him later, too. He's coming to the Silver Dragon for dinner."

Hmmm, thought Irma, *I didn't see Taranee with Nigel, either. I must have been gone by then, too.*

"So what happened?" Irma asked. "Don't keep us in suspense. Spill!"

Taranee shrugged. "My mom's had a change of heart about Nigel, thanks to my dad. And I'm pretty sure my brother helped. He always did like Nigel."

Irma sighed, thinking of Taranee's big brother. "Peter is such a hottie."

Taranee checked her watch once again. "He's coming by here to pick me up. Then we're going to rent a video and head back home together. I want to get back before Nigel shows."

"Excuse me?" said Irma, eagerly leaning forward across the table. "Did you say Peter's coming by the diner?"

What a convenient coincidence! Irma thought with glee. He always seemed to make Cornelia so nervous, and she was going to arrive at any minute.

Irma loved to watch a good potential romance unfold. She just wished there were one starring her! Sure, that cute new boy had given her the eye, but when she'd followed him, nothing had come of it.

And Martin Tubbs didn't count! Irma had dated the prince of geeks once—under pressure from her unbelievably bossy mother—but now they were just friends.

Thank goodness! she thought.

Peter, on the other hand, was the king of cool. He was pretty laid back, but Irma figured he'd probably be more interested in Cornelia. She got all the cute ones—without even trying! Peter was handsome, with chiseled features, a totally manly goatee, and big, long-lashed, caramel-colored eyes. He wore his hair in super-stylin' dreadlocks and slouched in doorways with the confident ease of a secret agent.

Yeah, she thought, Peter is totally hot. Plus, he has an awesome music collection, and he surfs. How cool is that?

Irma *had* to get the 411 on the guy if he was coming by that night. It might turn out to be an interesting meeting if Cornelia really did show up as planned.

"So . . ." she said, turning to Taranee, "what's going on with your big brother's social life these days? He doesn't have a girlfriend yet, does he?"

Just then, Irma felt Hay Lin nudge her in the ribs.

"Ow!" Irma squawked. "What did I say?"

"You know Cornelia is a little attracted to Peter," Hay Lin said in a hushed tone.

"Cornelia?" Irma made a show of looking all around the diner. "I don't see Cornelia here. Do you?" Irma flipped her hair. "And anyway, I was just asking *for* Corny. She should go out with him!"

"Come on, Irma," said Will. "Stop clowning around. Cornelia will be here soon. She is the one who called this emergency meeting. The weather probably just slowed her down. I'm sure she'll be here any minute—at least, I hope so."

"Why? What are you doing tonight?" Irma asked. "As if I can't guess."

Will smiled and shrugged. "Matt and I are getting together. We'll either catch a movie or just hang out at my place."

"Nice," said Taranee.

"Like your brother," Irma pressed.

Taranee shook her head. "Irma, I thought you were already interested in that new kid, the blond upperclassman. He was checking you out, and you looked like you were totally crushin' on him earlier today."

"That's right, she was," Will agreed. She turned to Irma. "You even ditched us to follow him. What happened?"

Irma waved her hand. "Don't ask. Some things are just *not* meant to be."

Will arched an eyebrow behind her shaggy

red bangs. "You followed him right to his girl-friend's house, didn't you?"

Irma sighed. "A guy should not be checking out *other* girls when he's already got one. Plus, he should be forced to wear a sign, you know? 'I'm taken.' It would really make life easier for me!"

Just then, Cornelia arrived.

She slipped into the booth and dropped her wet umbrella onto the floor. Irma was about to say something about Peter coming, but Cornelia wasn't interested in boy talk. She barely said hello before she started lecturing them all.

"Everything is clear to me now," Cornelia told her best friends. "Listen to me carefully. . . ."

Irma *tried* to listen carefully. She really did. But the more Corny talked, the less sense she made!

"Nerissa was able to get the essence of pure evil to seep out of the Heart of Candracar," Cornelia explained hurriedly, barely pausing to breathe. "And we were protected by the barriers of the ethereal shield that was generated by the Star of Cassidy. . . ."

Uh . . . right, thought Irma. And *this* is why we're all sitting here on this unbelievably soggy night?

The weather had turned really ugly. Even now, lightning flashed and thunder rumbled. Sheets of water poured down outside the diner's picture windows.

"We were all there when the essence of evil covered up the Temple, the Oracle, and the Elders of the Congregation. . . ."

As Cornelia rattled on, Irma glanced at the clock behind the counter.

Man, this is boring, she thought. It's a good thing I ordered a chocolate shake. Considering this tall tale of Corny's, I'll need the caffeine to keep from dozing!

With a quiet sigh, she lifted her paper cup and took a long sip of the cold drink.

"Then we passed out," said Cornelia, "but the Star of Cassidy must have transported us to Heatherfield. . . ."

Irma wasn't surprised that she had trouble paying attention. Miss Popular always loved to take charge of things and speak her mind on issues that affected W.I.T.C.H. But Irma remained mystified by *what* Corny was saying.

Irma glanced at the rest of the group, wondering how they were all taking it. They all seemed just as confused as she did. Hay Lin was scratching her head. Will looked mildly puzzled. Taranee's brow was furrowed, but she was listening intently, as if she were going to be tested on the material.

"Caleb was with us inside the shield," Cornelia told them. "I just hope he at least managed to get back to Meridian before it was too late!" At last, she stopped to take a breath and finally seemed to notice the perplexed expressions her friends were wearing. "Why are you all looking at me like that?" she asked, her voice tight with tension. "Don't you get it? It's all so clear!"

Will leaned forward and met Cornelia's gaze. "What's clear?"

"Losing our powers and forgetting our roles!" cried Cornelia. She threw up her hands, almost knocking over Will's soda. "Candracar doesn't exist anymore. I know it's hard to believe, but there's no other explanation, and—"

"Cornelia!" Will interrupted. She reached out and touched her arm. "You're obviously upset by something. But I'm having a hard time following you, so . . . um . . ."

"What?" Cornelia asked.

Will glanced around the table again—this time she was looking for support. Irma nodded her encouragement. So did Hay Lin and Taranee. It was obvious to Irma that Will was just saying what the rest of the girls were thinking.

"I . . . um . . ." Will continued. "I think I have to ask you a few questions."

"Oh," said Cornelia. Her tense face seemed to relax, and she leaned back. "Okay, what do you want to know?"

Will scratched her head. "Well, for starters . . . What's Candracar?"

A dead silence fell over the table for a few seconds. Then Cornelia's face seemed to fill with a combination of outrage and anger.

"No!" she shouted.

Leaping to her feet, Cornelia thumped the table with both palms, this time actually knocking over Will's soda. The brown liquid spilled out and formed a sticky puddle on the table.

"Tell me you're joking!" she screamed.

It was as if a fire had exploded in the middle of the diner. Every customer stopped talking and stared at the girls' table.

Irma blinked. She didn't embarrass easily, but she could feel her face flaming red. She didn't even have a good comeback. Her jaw went slack along with everybody else's.

Taranee's eyes grew wider than the frames of her glasses. And Hay Lin froze in midsip, the drinking straw still between her lips.

Will was the first one to find her voice. "Cornelia, we're your friends," she said softly. She stood and reached out to touch Cornelia's arm. "Even if we don't get what you're saying—"

"Stay away from me!" Cornelia cried. She jerked away from Will's touch, her face a twisted mixture of fury and hurt. Then she turned and ran toward the door.

"Wait!" Will called. She picked up Cornelia's umbrella and tried to follow her. But Cornelia was beyond consoling. She wheeled and shouted, "Don't come near me! . . . Don't . . ."

Cornelia's voice trailed off as she choked on her own tears. Then she turned and ran out.

Wow, Irma thought. She couldn't believe that asking a simple question like "What's

Candracar?" would make Cornelia totally freak like that.

Honestly, Irma couldn't figure out what Candracar was, either. Was it a new video game or TV show? Or was Cornelia just rehearsing for a drama-club production?

A play! Irma realized. That's got to be it, especially the way she stormed out of here. She must have been performing some sort of acting exercise. After all, Corny always was a drama queen!

EIGHT

Still sobbing uncontrollably, Cornelia burst through the diner's front doors and out into the stormy night.

All around her, the storm was still raging. Thunder echoed across Heatherfield's skyline. Wind rattled signs and whipped at tree branches. And roiling dark clouds dumped buckets of water, turning the wide city streets into fast-moving rivers.

Seeing the downpour, Cornelia stopped. She thought about going back inside for her umbrella, but she decided to wait out the worst of the storm under the awning.

The small metal canopy, however, provided little protection from the raging tempest. The blowing rain splattered her long checkered skirt and short gray jacket. The sidewalk puddles were ruining her new suede boots.

Cornelia barely noticed. Hugging herself, she shook her head, her warm tears mingling with icy raindrops as they streaked down her cheeks.

Everything, she thought. They've forgotten everything! I'm the only one left who knows the truth!

Cornelia liked to think of herself as a strong person. She had gone through a lot over the past year and a half. She'd learned to accept being a Guardian, to face evil with courage, and to come through for a friend.

But this revelation was almost too much for her to stand. Her best friends had forgotten the magic that bound them together as a powerful team; they'd forgotten the duty they had to the worlds they'd agreed to protect.

Cornelia felt abandoned now . . . lost. Her heart beat rapidly. She felt as if she were falling through a dark tunnel—and she didn't know where it would dump her. She closed her eyes and realized that she'd felt that way once before in her life, when she'd gone through that portal by herself.

Water had been swirling around her then, too. Powerful currents had thrust her forward, toward another world, with a force she had never experienced before.

Cornelia felt now as she had then, frightened and desperately missing the other Guardians. She missed Taranee, for her good sense and warming fire. She missed Hay Lin for her carefree laughter and bursts of soothing air. She even missed bigmouthed Irma, who might have been able to calm this raging rain! But most of all, she missed Will, for her fierce strength, the reassurance she offered, and the Heart, which Will controlled.

Cornelia couldn't stop sobbing. She had no idea where to turn. And she was terrified she'd end up the way she had when she'd gone through the portal that day in Metamoor—almost drowning in a deep pool she hadn't seen coming.

"Cornelia!"

Someone with a deep voice called her name. She looked up to find a tall boy loping down the soggy sidewalk. As he approached her, the bright windows of the diner illuminated the chiseled features of his handsome face. Cornelia instantly recognized him.

"Peter?" she murmured. It was Taranee's brother. But what was he doing there? she wondered.

She had always liked Peter. Once, she'd even dreamed about his holding her hand and becoming her boyfriend. He was kind and intelligent, and his laid-back manner made everyone feel comfortable around him.

Peter threw Cornelia an easy smile. "Everything okay?" he asked. "You seem pretty upset." He tilted his umbrella to shelter her from the wind and rain.

Cornelia felt Peter's warmth, his sturdiness as he moved closer. He had a strong surfer's body and a genuine charisma. Almost immediately, she felt a pull of attraction.

But I don't *want* to feel that, she thought.

"It's . . . it's nothing," Cornelia told him. "If you're looking for your sister, she's inside the diner."

"Great," said Peter. "I have to talk to her about tonight. Nigel's coming over, and my mom asked me to pick up a movie, so I . . ."

Cornelia felt lulled by the charm of Peter's deep, melodic voice. She found herself hoping he'd invite her to come along with him and Taranee.

You don't need to feel so alone, a voice inside her whispered. *You don't need to feel swamped by your worries. Peter's right here in front of you. . . . He likes you . . . and you like him, too. Why not give up, give in, forget . . . ?*

Cornelia found herself staring into Peter's eyes. They were so warm, so friendly, so inviting. A girl could get lost in those eyes, she realized.

Why worry about Candracar? the voice inside her continued. *Isn't it easier to forget all those other worlds so far away? Isn't it easier to forget Caleb?*

Caleb? she repeated. Then she blinked. Wait a second, she thought. What's happening here?

Shaking her head to clear it, Cornelia realized she couldn't stand that close to Peter for another second. Without saying a word to him, she ran off, down the wet sidewalk, half blinded by the drenching rain.

"Cornelia?" Peter called after her. "What's

wrong? Was it something I said?"

There was no explaining, and Cornelia didn't try. She just kept running through the dark downpour, tears of confusion and fear flowing from her eyes.

I almost drowned again, she thought. Just like when I went through that portal! But this time it wasn't in a bottomless fountain on another world. This time it was in the deep brown of Peter's eyes.

Instantly, Cornelia understood how her best friends had sunk into forgetfulness. As soon as they saw the boys they liked, they'd started to forget about their magical selves. They started to forget who they really were . . . Hay Lin and Eric; Taranee and Nigel; Irma and that blond upperclassman; Will and Matt!

And now . . . and now it's my turn, Cornelia realized.

Still shaken and scared, she raced through the dark, wet Heatherfield streets. She could feel the rain drenching her. Her wool skirt was absorbing water and growing heavier. Her new suede boots were far from waterproof. They were squishing with every step.

She tried desperately to remember Caleb.

But instead of his face, she saw Peter's! She could feel something inside her, some force trying to wash her mind.

Caleb, not Peter! she told herself over and over, fighting the forgetfulness. Caleb, not Peter! Caleb, not Peter! Caleb!

Broooommmm!

The booming thunder jolted her heart, and she raced even faster. She frantically looked around and realized she was only a few blocks from her apartment building. Picking up her long skirt, she ran as fast as she could to get there.

The doorman looked alarmed when he saw her. He anxiously asked her if she was okay.

Yeah, no, *duh,* she thought. I'm breathing hard, soaked to the bone, and leaving a slime trail wherever I walk.

She ignored him, rushed to the elevator, and repeatedly poked the call button until the doors opened. When the car reached the penthouse level, she raced across the thick hall carpeting and lunged at her family's carved mahogany front door.

Her mother was on the sofa reading a book, her legs primly crossed, her tasteful designer glasses perched on the end of her nose. Her father was crossing toward his study. He'd changed out of his banker's suit into a cashmere sweater and slacks. In his hand was a cherrywood pipe. Both of them looked up when Cornelia burst in, letting the door bang against the wall of the entryway.

Her parents both stared speechlessly at their sopping-wet daughter. Classical music played softly on the state-of-the-art sound system.

Cornelia grimaced. Her parents stared at her as if she'd brought the raging storm with her, right into the middle of their living room.

Well, too bad, she thought. I can't go through any clueless parental grilling right now. I just *can't*! So I guess I'll have to answer their questions before they can ask them.

"Yes, Dad, I am drenched!" she cried. "Yes, Mom, I did forget my umbrella! I'm not hungry, so leave me alone!"

Still sopping wet, she stomped across the living room, down the hall, and to her bedroom.

Oh, perfect, she thought, swinging open the door. Her six-year-old sister, Lilian, was sitting at Cornelia's desk, drawing stick figures and rainbows on Cornelia's personal, engraved stationery. The earth Guardian fumed.

I told the little toad not to mess with my private stuff! Cornelia silently raged.

Lilian looked up and stuck out her tongue. She obviously couldn't have cared less that she'd been caught misbehaving.

I *cannot* deal with this right now, Cornelia thought. Clenching her fists and closing her eyes, she shouted, "Don't say one single word, Lilian! Just get out of my room, and stay out!"

The little girl seemed too shocked to speak. She quickly got up and hurried past Cornelia and out of the room.

Slam!

Cornelia collapsed against the door. With Lilian gone, she was finally alone and beginning to feel sorry that she'd had to subject her family to a tantrum.

"Grouchy and mean-tempered," she murmured. "Everybody thinks I'm like that. Everybody except my friends . . . But pretty soon, they'll all be on their dates."

Cornelia's head began to throb, and she

closed her eyes. She could see them all, laughing and talking at the diner.

They were all very happy, she realized. But that was only because they were oblivious. They had forgotten everything that had happened in Candracar! They had forgotten their lives as Guardians.

"And once they go off on their dates," she whispered, "they'll completely forget even the last traces of the magic that kept us together. . . ."

Tears welled up in her eyes again, and she turned toward the door of her bedroom, pressing her wet cheek against the smooth, cool wood.

"Oh, Mom and Dad, I wish I could tell you all about what I'm going through," Cornelia quietly rasped. "You always used to help me understand things. . . ."

But this was something they would never understand. Only her best friends knew what it was like to have magic deep inside oneself. Only they knew what it felt like to soar on powerful wings, wield elemental magic, and travel to other dimensions.

But now, even they had forgotten.

Cornelia was the only one who remembered. But what good was remembering, when she no longer had use of her special gift . . . the gift of being able to transform herself into a person braver and more powerful than she had ever thought she could be!

She squeezed her eyes shut once more, feeling scared and empty and alone. She was beginning to lose all hope. She tried to see herself as a Guardian again, strong and powerful, courageous enough to say, "Bring it on!" to the blackest heart in the universe.

But she couldn't see herself like that anymore. The image had turned fuzzy. . . . It was fading! She was already forgetting!

She desperately tried to remember Caleb. She reached deep into her mind to resurrect his face. But she could recall only Peter!

"No," she whispered, horrified. "It's happening to me, too. I'm going to be just like the others. I'm going to forget everything . . . but I can't forget Caleb. Not Caleb!"

Frantic, she wheeled away from the door and paced through the room, thumping her head with her palm, trying to will herself to recall Caleb's image. Then her eyes fell on her desk, and she stopped dead. Right there in a messy pile sat the rough drawings her little sister had been making.

"A drawing!" Cornelia cried. "That's it! That's how it all began, when my friend Elyon drew a picture of the boy from my dreams. . . ."

Cornelia yanked open her desk drawers, one after another, frantically searching each one.

"Elyon's drawing . . . It's got to be here!"

Finally, she saw it: the thick paper from Elyon's sketch pad, rolled up and tied with a red ribbon, just as on the day Elyon had given it to her . . .

Cornelia had been so happy and excited that day. She'd placed third in her first figure-skating competition. It had been very special, because Elyon had been right there to cheer her on and see her awarded the bronze medal.

"*You've told me so much about him,*" Elyon had said when she gave Cornelia the picture. "*I feel like I've already met him.*"

But there was one thing Elyon had said she didn't understand. She didn't get why Cornelia was so stubborn about waiting for her dream boy.

Elyon had actually tried to convince her to

go out with another boy. *"While you're looking for your imaginary prince, you could still hang with Pete,"* she'd told Cornelia. *"He's a really great guy."*

Even then, Cornelia knew deep inside that her imaginary prince, the boy of her dreams, would appear one day in her life.

"I have room for only one great love," she'd told Elyon. *"And I don't want anyone but him. . . ."*

With shaking hands, Cornelia now sat on the edge of her bed. She untied the red string and unfurled the drawing.

"Caleb!" she cried, at last seeing the image of his sweet face. "Caleb!"

Every feature she loved was there. "Your mouth, your eyes . . . I can see them," she whispered, running her hands over every line. "I can touch them."

His sad green eyes; his strong, square jaw; his shaggy brown hair; even his dusty rebel coat and determined expression were there.

Hugging the drawing close to her chest, she closed her eyes again, but this time her memories came flooding back in torrents. Every moment they'd shared was made real to her again—the day he'd rescued her from that fountain in Metamoor; their struggle together to free his world from the evil Prince Phobos; their fight to stay together time and time again.

And with that flood of memories, her love for him filled her to the brim, showering her with strength, renewing her belief in that magical part of herself.

This time, when she opened her eyes, she was no longer in her bedroom. She was no longer in Heatherfield. She wasn't even on the earth!

She blinked and rubbed her eyes. The drawing was no longer in her hands. She looked down to find she was now dressed in her purple and turquoise Guardian clothes. She moved her muscles and felt the flutter of wings on her back. Her limbs were longer, leaner, and more powerful. And she felt her tingling magic surging through her again, pulsing with an intense power that almost overwhelmed her.

Glancing quickly around, she saw that Caleb was by her side. Her dream boy was *real*—but, for some reason, he was *sleeping*. Everyone was! Like Caleb, Irma, Taranee, Hay

Lin, and Will were floating inside the ethereal shield, fast asleep.

I've woken up in Candracar, Cornelia thought. My body never left! But what happened to me and the others? Was it a spell? What is going on?

She moved to the edge of her transparent cage, pressed her palms against the wall of the shield, and peered out—to find Nerissa peering right back.

NINE

"Cornelia's woken up!" Nerissa cried. "The spell has been broken!"

For centuries, Nerissa had been yearning to destroy Candracar. And finally, *finally*, her wish was coming true! After cracking open the Heart, she'd used her vengeful hate to transform the orb's core energy into the essence of evil.

Now the thick, black ooze flowed out of the gashed crystal, staining everything with its poison. Like living tentacles, the gunk twisted and curled down the Temple columns, strangling everything it touched. The slithering goo rained onto the floor of the Temple and pooled in a lake of infinite darkness.

Already, the Heart's black lake was

high enough to cover the heads of the meditating Oracle and Elders. Soon the toxic fluid would blot out the glorious Temple entirely, and Candracar itself would be sent into oblivion.

All along, Nerissa had known that the only force that could stop her was that of those five little brats with wings! That was why she'd assaulted them with a very special enchantment.

My spell *should* have taken care of the Guardians for good, she thought. But Cornelia's memories of Caleb were too strong. And now that she's awakened, that blasted little blonde is waking all the other Guardians!

Inside her own ethereal shield, Nerissa shook her fist in fury and cried, "I can't believe she broke the spell!"

"I don't understand," said Shagon.

Nerissa turned to face the shaggy-haired giant standing beside her. Sky-blue armor covered his supernatural muscles. Long yellow hair framed the blank, puppetlike mask that was his face.

Nerissa had created Shagon to carry out her every command. Of course, at times, she was confounded by his stubborn human soul, which caused him to question her at the most inconvenient times.

She had to admit, Shagon simply was not as obedient as her other servants.

Khor, for instance, was a delightfully ferocious beast who always obeyed her commands. But what else *would* you expect from a mutt? Nerissa thought.

Originally, Khor had been Shagon's dog, his faithful, furry friend. When Nerissa had seen the mutt sniffing around her lair on Mount Thanos, she'd zapped him with her dark magic. Khor had instantly changed from friendly, lovable pet to cutthroat beast with fangs, claws, and vicious attitude.

After Nerissa had transformed the animal, his geologist owner had come looking for him. In need of more servants, she'd decided to claim the geologist, too.

Now both her servants—man and beast—awaited her bidding inside the ethereal shield. Two other creations, Ember and Tridart, also stood ready to serve her.

Ember was a female demon. She had been fashioned out of the volcanic fires inside Nerissa's mountain tomb. Tridart was an iceman. Nerissa had sculpted him from the glacial ice around the tomb.

Of all her servants, however, Shagon was the most powerful. To him she had given an undefeatable talent. Shagon drew strength from the emotion of hatred. The more hatred an opponent expressed for Shagon during a battle, the stronger Shagon became. Nerissa had been relying on that strength since the day she'd transformed him.

Now, however, Shagon was just being annoying, pestering her with questions. "Why did she open her eyes?" he asked.

"Blame it on love, Shagon," Nerissa replied with disgust, watching Cornelia shower Caleb with kisses.

"Love?" Shagon asked.

"Yes," spat Nerissa. "She woke up because of that wretched, unbearable emotion."

Nerissa had never understood love. That silly sentiment might have awakened Cornelia, but it was a losing strategy. In Nerissa's view, love was a scam. It weakened people, it made them vulnerable, and it required sacrifice.

How absurd! she thought. You'd have to be a fool to think that love had any benefits!

Hate was what Nerissa understood. Now *there's* an emotion to live by, she thought.

The power of hate was like nothing else. It had given Nerissa the strength for her long, vengeful mission of reclaiming the Heart and destroying Candracar.

Hate is what allowed me to turn that geologist into my servant Shagon, she thought, and his dog into the beast Khor. Hate is what will allow me to defeat my opponents and emerge victorious!

"Cornelia is waking the other Guardians up!" Tridart cried. He pointed his icy finger at the Guardians' shield.

Nerissa threw a disgusted look over at the dim-witted iceman. "I can see that, Tridart!" she snapped. That chilly head of his must have frozen his brains, she thought. "This wasn't supposed to happen!"

Just then, Nerissa noticed Will rubbing her eyes and shaking her head, as if to clear it. Then the little Keeper turned to Cornelia.

Nerissa could see that Will was about to speak. And the sorceress wanted to hear what she had to say. So she raised her hand, silently commanding her servants to *shut up!*

"Now I remember!" Will told Cornelia. "The Oracle . . . the Heart being broken! What was going on back in Heatherfield?"

"I don't know," Cornelia replied, putting a hand on Will's shoulder. "Maybe it was all a dream. Another one of Nerissa's nightmares."

Nerissa gritted her teeth, impatient with their stupidity.

"No, girls!" she shouted at them through the transparent walls. "Your bodies were here, but your minds were back in Heatherfield!"

Will and Cornelia turned to face Nerissa. So did Irma, Hay Lin, and Taranee.

All of the Guardians, obviously, were waiting for an explanation. And Nerissa was only too happy to enlighten them. It's the least I can do, she cackled to herself, since I'm about to destroy them!

"Before coming to Candracar, you created perfect doubles of yourselves," she said. "You thought you were safe inside the shield, but my magic got through . . . and it made you fall into a deep sleep. Then I transferred your minds into the bodies of your astral drops."

Will frowned. "Then . . . what we lived through in Heatherfield was . . ."

"*Real life*, Will," Nerissa informed her. "Nothing should have made you see through my little trick!"

Irma's jaw dropped. "If that's true, it means the new boy in town actually did give me the eye!"

"And my mom really saw me kiss Nigel!" cried Taranee, looking stunned.

"Everything was going perfectly," Nerissa continued. "Even Kadma helped me out . . . unwittingly."

Cornelia stepped forward. "How?"

"When Candracar was swallowed up in my dark force, her Eternal Gift temporarily faded away. Without that last trace of her powers, she was convinced that the Temple no longer existed. Poor old fool!"

Will threw up her hands. "You trapped our minds in the bodies of our astral drops!" she cried. "That explains everything."

Taranee nodded. "It sure does. And we were powerless, because our astral drops don't have any powers!"

Nerissa smirked at the girls. "If you ask me, you should work on your astral drops. They've got poor memories, and they're quite gullible."

It truly was amazing, thought Nerissa, how easily the Guardians were distracted. One boy here and one boy there, and they were all little goners—well, *almost* all.

Nerissa cursed Cornelia and her wretched love for that silly boy from Metamoor. If only the little blonde hadn't found that drawing, she thought, she surely would have forgotten her identity, too.

"You were the one who confused us!" Cornelia cried, angrily pressing her palms against the shield's invisible wall.

"Yes," said Nerissa with a wicked laugh. "But your friends did seem to enjoy my little trick."

Nerissa was amazed at how easy it had been to unsettle the girls. All she'd done was make them believe that they no longer possessed magic. Without that magic, they could barely remember the reason they all were friends!

"You're such a coward!" Cornelia shouted. "Why didn't you take us on face to face? Were you afraid of us?"

The smirk on Nerissa's face suddenly vanished.

Blast you and your love, silly Guardian,

she thought, cursing Cornelia again.

The sleeping spell had been working. And because the Guardians' minds and thoughts were back in Heatherfield, the ethereal shield protecting them in Candracar had been growing weaker. It wouldn't have been long before Nerissa could have penetrated its transparent walls. Then she would simply have done away with the Guardians in their sleep.

Too bad I'll actually have to make an effort now to destroy those brats, she thought. It's a shame, really . . . obliterating the Guardians won't be nearly as easy as I'd hoped. But, what the heck? I've waited an eternity for this moment. A good old-fashioned rumble might actually be amusing.

After all, she reasoned, my four dark servants make up a force that cannot be conquered. With them by my side *and* with the Heart of Candracar under my control, I cannot fail. . . .

And yet Nerissa could not deny that Will and the rest of the Guardians had been able to escape her spells in the past—and defeat her servants.

"You're not strong enough. . . ." Will had

once impudently warned Nerissa.

And now Cornelia, the cheeky little earth Guardian, was echoing that infuriating taunt. *A coward*, Nerissa repeated to herself in a cold rage. *Afraid . . .*

Perhaps, in the deepest, darkest part of herself, Nerissa did secretly fear that Cornelia and Will were right. But never, in a million centuries, would she ever admit it!

I'll show you who's afraid, you little brats, she thought as her bright blue eyes began to glow with rage. Yes, it's time to get down to business. . . . It's time to annihilate every last one of you Guardians and destroy Candracar forever!

TEN

Hay Lin stepped up to the edge of the ethereal shield and peered hard into the depths of the Temple.

While the Guardians had been under Nerissa's sleeping spell, things had gotten worse in Candracar. Everything in the Temple had been swallowed up by Nerissa's black slime. *Everything!*

The glistening crystal columns, the endless majestic hallways and jeweled floors . . . all of it was blotted out. Only the highest windows were visible above the pool of muck, but Hay Lin could see nothing beyond them. Their crystal-clear glass had been splattered with the supernatural ooze.

Did the brilliant blue sky and

fluffy white clouds of Candracar still exist beyond the darkened windows? Hay Lin wondered. Or had the black rain from the broken Heart obliterated them, too?

Before Nerissa had begun her attack, Hay Lin's grandmother had been sitting in the center of the Temple's ornate floor, having joined the Oracle and the Elders of the Congregation in a meditation circle.

Hay Lin pressed her face against the transparent cage. She looked for any sign of her beloved grandmother. But all she could see was the vile whirlpool of tarlike fluid that had swallowed Yan Lin up.

Hay Lin covered her mouth. I can't believe it, she thought. My grandmother is somewhere under that evil rot!

When Hay Lin had first seen her grandmother disappear, she had screamed and cried and beaten the walls of the ethereal shield. But Hay Lin didn't feel hysterical any longer. She didn't feel confused or lost. After waking from Nerissa's spell, what Hay Lin felt was stonecold furious!

The Guardian trained her almond-shaped eyes on the sorceress across the hall. Nerissa was leering at the Guardians from inside her own ethereal shield.

Cornelia is right, Hay Lin decided. Nerissa is so sneaky, so low, she nearly destroyed us with a nasty trick. She couldn't even handle a fair fight! She *is* a coward.

But you made a mistake, Nerissa, thought Hay Lin. You put our minds in our astral drops' bodies to make us believe our powers were gone. But here's the four-one-one. You didn't weaken me. You made me stronger!

Like anyone who loses something, then finds it again, Hay Lin valued her magic now more than ever. She was intensely aware of the dazzling energy singing inside her body. Like a living, electric river, it pulsed and sparked through her veins.

Just then, Hay Lin noticed Will turning to the rest of W.I.T.C.H. A look of understanding was on the Keeper's face. "Remember what the Oracle said after the ethereal shield surrounded us?" Will asked the girls. *"If you allow yourselves to be distracted, the shield will weaken."*

Hay Lin nodded, remembering where her own mind had wandered—thanks to Nerissa. Like the four other Guardians, she had been magically transported back to Heatherfield.

Of course, at the time, Hay Lin hadn't known that her mind had been put inside her astral drop. She only knew that her magic was completely gone.

Then she'd seen Eric Lyndon, the boy she'd had a crush on for the past few months. His lanky form and kind, intelligent eyes had practically cast a spell on Hay Lin, making her forget that she was a Guardian. She had talked and talked with Eric during their long walk to Heatherfield Park. And she'd laughed with him as they'd cleaned up the mess inside the observatory's main hall and the basement planetarium.

In the form of her astral drop, Hay Lin had failed to remember what had caused that mess. Her memories had vanished into a fuzzy haze. Now, however, she remembered everything. Now Hay Lin knew why the observatory had been trashed.

The night before, Will had wanted to look for the Star of Cassidy. So the Guardians had gone with her to break into the observatory. Using the telescope, they'd found the Star. But Nerissa had sensed what was happening. And she'd sent her servant Khor to attack the girls viciously.

With the help of Cassidy's Star, W.I.T.C.H. had defeated the beast. But the struggle hadn't been pretty. Khor had put up a strong fight, and they had left the observatory and planetarium a wreck. That was why Eric had welcomed Hay Lin's help in cleaning it up. And, since Hay Lin was crushin' on him big-time, she had hastily volunteered.

Hay Lin had enjoyed spending time with Eric. He was such a great and sweet guy. She'd felt totally carefree for the first time in ages. Her worries had seemed to vanish, along with the burden of being a Guardian.

But something important had vanished with all of that, Hay Lin realized. It was hard to name, but it was unmistakable. It was that special, confident feeling her magic had given her.

Hay Lin knew that she had been born with a gift. Although it had taken her some time to recognize it, that elemental magic had been a part of her spirit, a part of her identity, from the very beginning. And when it was taken away, she'd been left with a profound sense of emptiness.

That must have been why I went so boy crazy, she concluded. I thought Eric could replace my missing magic. I thought he could make me feel special. So I started to make him the center of my world. But now I know the truth.

"Nerissa only wanted to distract our thoughts from Candracar!" Hay Lin told the other Guardians.

The members of W.I.T.C.H. nodded. She could see the fire burning in Taranee's eyes. She could sense the storm clouds forming in Irma's.

"What a skunk!" Irma yelled. Then she said aloud what everyone else had already guessed. "The shield would've disappeared, and she'd have been able to do away with us in our sleep!"

Across the room, Nerissa rolled her eyes. Obviously, she thought the Guardians' idea of fair play ridiculous.

"Why fight an exhausting battle when you can easily wipe out your adversary by cheating?" asked the sorceress with a dismissive wave.

"And what a foolproof plan you had,

Nerissa," Irma drily retorted. "It's a shame we're awake now, and ready to teach you a lesson!"

Nerissa was about to respond. But something happened that left her momentarily speechless. Her ethereal shield began to move. Slowly, it floated across the vast Temple. But Nerissa hadn't commanded the Heart of Candracar to move it.

Just then, Hay Lin felt a jolt. The transparent cage around her and the other Guardians began to move, too. Hay Lin shot a glance over at Will, but the Keeper had a surprised look on her face. She hadn't asked the Star of Cassidy to move their shield, either!

The Heart of Candracar and the Star of Cassidy seemed to be attracting each other like magnets. The pull of the two orbs was dragging together the two ethereal shields protecting the two opposing forces.

With gaping mouths the Guardians watched their ethereal shield bear down on Nerissa's. Hay Lin could see that Nerissa herself looked surprised and angry. And her evil servants appeared confused, too.

Shagon, Khor, Tridart, and Ember were all

looking at their mistress for an explanation. But Nerissa had none. Her eyes were wide with outrage. Her mouth twisted in a terrible grimace.

"No!" she cried to the Heart. She raised her magic staff and angrily shook it. "I order you to stop!"

But the Heart didn't obey Nerissa's command. It appeared to be on its very own mission.

"Look!" exclaimed Will. "The Star of Cassidy and the Heart of Candracar are about to—"

Flash!

"Aaagh!" cried Hay Lin. As the two orbs suddenly crashed together, she shielded her eyes from the blinding light.

The other Guardians cried out, too. Then the scorching brightness faded. Hay Lin rubbed her eyes and peered beyond the shield. She couldn't believe it. The two magic orbs had become one! A single orb now floated in the middle of the Temple.

"They've accomplished their mission," said Will in awe. "That horrible black slime has stopped!"

Hay Lin could see that Will was right. The

Heart of Candracar was restored! It was no longer gashed. And it glowed like a star again. The Star of Cassidy had healed the broken Heart and stopped its gush of black rain!

"Whoa!" cried Hay Lin, feeling another jolt. "What was that?"

"The two shields are vanishing!" Taranee cried.

The transparent bubble surrounding the Guardians suddenly disappeared. As panic rose through her body, Hay Lin automatically began to flutter her wings to keep from falling into the pool of muck below. But what about her fellow Guardians?

As the air Guardian, Hay Lin was the only flier in the group. She quickly assessed the situation and knew that she had to use her powers to help her friends. She couldn't risk having them fall into the black ooze below. With all of her concentration, Hay Lin focused her concern on her fellow Guardians and gave them a great gift—the gift of flight!

"Wow!" Irma cried, testing out her new flying ability. One by one, each of the Guardians took to the air to avoid the ooze below.

Now all the Guardians were flying over the

evil ooze. Hay Lin was relieved and proud as she watched her friends soar. She flexed her colorful wings behind her. They had the power of a jet engine, the speed of a rocket. And she was itching to soar.

Cornelia took hold of Caleb to keep him from falling. She quickly transferred him to a ledge above the vile muck.

Then Hay Lin noticed that the shield holding Nerissa and her servants had melted away, too, and that they were out in the open now, just like the Guardians.

But what did it mean? Hay Lin wondered. What should we do now?

She looked at Will, along with Irma, Taranee, and Cornelia. Will was their leader, the Keeper. So whatever W.I.T.C.H. did next was up to her.

Will met the gaze of each of the Guardians. She clenched her fists and cried, "It's time to fight!"

Hay Lin nodded. With a deep breath, she reconnected with the stream of magical energy pulsing inside her. Then she narrowed her eyes on the sorceress and her creepy crew.

You know what, Nerissa? Hay Lin thought.

You tried to make us forget our magic, but you failed. I can feel my power over wind and currents. The power to call down a whirlwind with a wave of my arm. The power to summon a typhoon with the breath from my lungs.

I know who I am again. . . .

I am a part of W.I.T.C.H.!

I am the air Guardian!

I am not afraid!

And I'm ready to fight!

ELEVEN

Will felt as though she were hovering inside a cave. All around her, the eerie blackness of the slimed Temple absorbed every bit of light. And the Heart was the campfire burning at its center.

She gazed into the dazzling brilliance of the crystal orb floating between her and Nerissa. Now that the Star of Cassidy and Heart of Candracar had been united, the resulting pendant burned with the energy of a small sun. Will could hardly wait to reclaim that energy and unleash its power on the smirking sorceress levitating in front of her.

"You've planned things out well, Guardians," Nerissa hissed. Against the bleak background, her blue eyes seemed to glow in the bright light of the Heart. Her long hair appeared lustrous as it flowed down her silk-and-velvet gown.

Despite Nerissa's surprise at the Heart's behavior, she appeared as steadfast as ever. She clutched her magic staff so tightly Will expected lightning bolts to start flying out of it at any second.

"To each his own adversary, then!" Nerissa confidently declared.

You got it, thought Will. Each of the Guardians had already picked out a different rival to challenge.

Irma had chosen Ember. As the water Guardian, she was the perfect person to douse the fire sorceress back into a pile of ashes!

Taranee had picked out Tridart. The fire Guardian could hardly wait to melt the iceman down into a frosty puddle.

Cornelia and Caleb were ready to take on Shagon. They knew he was the master of hate. But together, with the strength of their love, they were prepared to bring him down.

Hay Lin looked more than eager for her grudge match against Khor. During that beast's assault on the Heatherfield Observatory, he had really knocked the air Guardian around. So it came as no surprise to Will that Hay Lin wanted to return the favor.

Finally, Will took aim at her very own opponent—Nerissa. "One lousy Keeper deserves another," Will quietly quipped.

Of course, W.I.T.C.H. didn't think of Will as a "lousy" Keeper. She knew that. But she still felt terrible about losing the Heart the way she had.

None of this would have happened if it hadn't been for me, she reminded herself. *I was stupid enough to let myself get tricked by Nerissa. I was stupid enough to let her make me doubt my friends and myself. And then I willingly gave her the Heart. . . . But all that's past now, and Nerissa has been tormenting us long enough!*

Already the sorceress had smothered the Oracle, the Elders, and Hay Lin's grandmother with foul-smelling slime. And she was about to annihilate Candracar. Some payback was definitely in order!

"But," Nerissa warned, "in this battle, it'll be the Heart of Candracar that makes all the difference. And it's still mine!"

The sorceress stretched out her hand and extended her power, calling the magic orb to her. The Heart began to move slowly toward the ancient Keeper.

But Will was a Keeper, too.

In Heatherfield, she'd felt empty and lost in her astral drop's body. Her magic had been totally gone.

Not anymore! When Will reached into her slender form this time, she could feel the magic pulsing through her. She stretched out her hand and focused her deeply rooted power, silently calling the Heart to her.

It worked! The tiny orb stopped moving in Nerissa's direction and began to move toward Will!

Will stifled a laugh at the shocked look on Nerissa's face. It appeared that Miss Congeniality hadn't expected to lose her control of the Heart.

"Get over here!" Nerissa shrieked. "Come back to your master!"

The Heart stopped moving toward Will. But it didn't move any closer to Nerissa, either. It simply continued hovering between Will and

Nerissa—the two Keepers.

"Maybe it's not quite sure yet who its real master is," Will told the outraged sorceress. With complete calm, she called on a new surge of magic, which she used to silently draw the Heart to her again.

Once more, the dazzling orb began to move, ever so slowly, toward Will.

Nerissa began to freak! "But it's mine!" she cried. "You gave it to me yourself!"

The evil sorceress concentrated all her power, and the Heart stopped moving toward Will. Again it reversed direction and began floating toward Nerissa.

"Only because you tricked me," Will shot back, concentrating her own power on the Heart.

The orb didn't reverse directions this time, but it did stop moving toward Nerissa. Now it simply hovered again as Will and Nerissa each tried hard to control it.

"Anyway, Nerissa," Will continued, "you'll have to ask Cassidy for it now! She was the one who gave it life. The same life that you destroyed years ago!"

Fury crossed Nerissa's face. Then, as if an

idea had occurred to her, she relaxed her features into a look of forced benevolence.

"Will," she said softly, "let me be the one to take the Heart. . . . You know I'm doing this for you."

"What?" Cornelia and Taranee cried out together.

"Did you hear that?" exclaimed Hay Lin.

"Yeah!" Irma replied. "At the Miss Lot-of-Nerve contest, she'd win first, second, and third prize!"

Will turned her head toward the Guardians chattering behind her. "Let her talk," she said. "I want to hear what she has to say."

"Yes, Will," Nerissa said, in a sickeningly sweet voice. "Listen to me, and think it over. Only the two of us know what it really means to bear the Heart and how difficult it is. . . ."

Will frowned, not liking where Nerissa was going with this.

"In Heatherfield," the sorceress continued, "inside the body of your astral drop, you got a taste of *real* life. An existence without powers, of course . . . but also without secrets. A happy, carefree life, with your mother, with dear Matt . . ."

Will's hand remained outstretched, but her concentration wavered. She felt her thoughts drifting back to her time in Heatherfield. She knew Nerissa's words were not to be trusted . . . but the sorceress was right.

The Oracle had put the Guardians in charge of fighting evil. They were supposed to protect not only Candracar and the earth but the entire universe. Will remembered how she'd struggled with that hefty responsibility. The Heart had indeed become a very heavy burden to carry.

The worst part of being the Keeper was *keeping* that very fact a secret from the people closest to her. Over time, it had worn down Will's nerves.

She had never gotten along very well with her mother. But not being able to tell her mom what was really happening in her life had really strained their relationship.

On the other hand, when Will was in her astral drop form, her relationship with her mom had felt almost perfect. They had laughed together at breakfast and dinner and felt completely carefree.

Will felt the same way about Matt.

In the form of her nonmagical double, she

had been truly happy with her boyfriend. They had biked across town together. Then she'd helped him feed the animals in his grandfather's pet store.

Without the Heart, there was nothing standing between them. No secrets. She had laughed and enjoyed herself as never before. He'd even made a date to see her again that evening.

Will still had doubts about carrying the Heart. She had screwed up. And she still wondered whether she could actually live up to the massive responsibility this placed on her shoulders.

Nerissa was obviously aware of Will's internal struggles. "I can relieve you of the heavy burden of your task," she cooed to Will.

The sorceress stretched out her arm and focused even more power, beckoning the orb closer. "Give me the Heart again, Will," she pleaded. "You deserve a *normal* life."

Will took a deep breath and then exhaled. She met Nerissa's glowing blue gaze.

"Maybe you *can* relieve me of the Heart's heavy burden," Will told the sorceress. "But that's not why I'm going to stop calling the Heart to me."

Hearing Will's words, the Guardians gasped in shock. They couldn't believe what Will was about to do.

Will withdrew her hand, along with her powerful magic. She released her hold on the Heart.

The floating Heart reversed its course. And once again, it began to move slowly in Nerissa's direction.

"Will! What's wrong?" cried Hay Lin.

"What are you doing?" demanded Irma.

But Will didn't turn around to answer her fellow Guardians. She remained still, her eyes fixed on the Heart.

Will wasn't afraid of Nerissa. And she wasn't giving up the fight, either. She'd simply remembered what the Oracle had told her.

Abide . . . by the decisions . . . of the Heart.

His words were as clear in Will's mind now as if he'd just spoken them aloud in her ear. And Will knew she had to listen. She had to pull back her power.

Right now, I'm sure Nerissa thinks that I'm giving up, thought Will. And, hey, my life just might be easier if I *weren't* the Keeper. It's a difficult destiny—one I might not have chosen for myself. But then, I guess, that's kind of the whole point of destiny, isn't it?

"Destiny is not something you choose," Hay Lin's grandmother had once told the Guardians. "It is something you must learn to accept."

Like the four dragons, Will recalled.

And in that moment, the ancient legend of the Heart's origin suddenly came back to her. The old Chinese story had told of four beautiful dragons—red, yellow, black, and pearl.

One day, those colorful dragons had heard the prayers of the poor starving people on the earth below. And they had swooped down from the sky to help them.

At first, the dragons went to the Jade Emperor. They asked him to provide rain for the people, so that their crops would not die and their starving might end.

The emperor was angry at being disturbed. But he told the dragons that he'd take care of the rain. Then he waved them away.

Ten days went by without rain. So the dragons got together and took care of the problem themselves. They flew down to the sea and scooped up water in their mouths. Then they flew high in the sky and sprayed the water into the clouds. The clouds rained down on the farmland, and the people were saved.

But the emperor was furious. He had the dragons arrested and brought to him in chains. To punish them for defying him, he ordered each of the beautiful dragons imprisoned in a mountain for eternity.

The mountain spirit claimed the red, yellow, black, and pearl dragons. Each was absorbed into a different mountain. But their punishment was so wrong, so unjust, that the powerful nymph Xin Jing appeared before the Jade Emperor in a flash of light.

"Your cruelty is equaled only by your arrogance," she told the emperor. Xin Jing could not restore the dragons to their former lives. But she could free their spirits from their mountain prisons.

So she released the dragons' spirits into the countryside, where they became four flowing rivers. Then she disappeared. All that was left of the nymph was a beautiful crystal amulet. That amulet contained her essence and those of the four dragons.

"Heart of Crystal," whispered Will. That

was what the name Xin Jing meant. And if the Heart of Candracar truly held the spirit of the magical nymph Xin Jing, then it was a thinking entity and would ultimately choose what it believed was the just path.

I am doing the right thing, Will assured herself. I must stop trying to control the Heart and accept whatever destiny comes. . . .

TWELVE

It's official, Irma decided. Will has gone mental.

What other explanation was there for what she'd just done?

The struggle over the new-and-improved Heart had been going full steam ahead. Will had been holding her own against the queen of slime. But then Will had quit, just like that. For some reason, Will had released her end of the tug-of-war magic!

Okay, thought Irma, so Will's life as Keeper hasn't exactly been a picnic. Carrying the Heart has gotten her into trouble at school, at home, and with her boyfriend . . . not to mention with the occasional other-worldly creature! And, of course, leading the Guardians isn't always a tea party.

But Will must have figured out what Irma had discovered already. Life without magic totally reeked!

In Heatherfield, without her water magic, Irma had felt like a complete scatterbrain inside her astral drop. She had no sense of direction whatsoever! She'd actually wasted her time following that hot new boy all the way to his girlfriend's house!

Ugh. Who needs that aggravation? Irma asked herself. Not me. I want my water magic to be there for me, centering me. I want to feel like I'm a part of something important, something that matters. Without W.I.T.C.H., I felt completely unfocused, totally lost.

Didn't Will feel that way, too? Irma wondered. Did she really believe a "normal" life, a life without magic, was better?

Nerissa truly was powerful. Her easy-pour-evil trick had made a royal mess of Candracar, and she'd almost destroyed the Guardians. But had she really been able to trick Will into giving up the Heart a *second* time?

Irma was just about to leap forward and shake some sense into Will when she heard the girl speak. And thank goodness, Irma thought, Will's words explained what she was doing. . . .

"Deciding who should get that pendant is an act as presumptuous as you are, Nerissa," Will told the sorceress. "The Heart of Candracar isn't a mere object, but a thinking entity, just like you and me. It's the spirit of the nymph Xin Jing. . . ."

Xin Jing, Irma repeated to herself. Omigosh! The story of the four dragons!

Irma glanced at Hay Lin, and they exchanged hopeful looks. Clearly, Will remembered the ancient legend that Nerissa had forgotten.

"It's not the Keeper who chooses the Heart," Will reminded Nerissa, "but the other way around."

Now I get it, thought Irma. The Heart will see that Will's strength flows from her belief and trust in her four friends—the four dragons. Nerissa, on the other hand, *lost* her belief in her friends and fellow Guardians. She betrayed them all and even murdered one of them.

But would the Heart really be able to sense the difference between the two Keepers?

Nerissa's hand was still outstretched. The

strain on her face was extreme. She was obviously ignoring Will. She was using every bit of her energy to control the Heart.

All of the Guardians held their breath, waiting for the Heart to make its decision. At first, it began to drift toward Nerissa's strong pull, but then it hesitated. For what seemed like an eternity, it hovered in place. And then it changed direction and quickly floated right into Will's hands!

"Yes!" Hay Lin shouted. "Way to go!"

"You did it!" Taranee exclaimed.

"Good job!" Cornelia cried.

"Whew!" Irma said, glancing at the other Guardians. "For a moment there, I thought Will had gone nuts."

Just a few feet away, Nerissa's crew of evil servants began muttering in confusion. Then Irma saw Tridart step forward.

"What should we do, Nerissa?" he asked. "Do we attack them?"

Nerissa was shaking so badly with rage she looked ready to explode. "Silence, you stupid chunk of ice!" she screamed. "Things have changed."

Irma stood ready with the other Guardians,

waiting to see what Nerissa would do next. Without the Heart, the sorceress didn't stand much chance of winning. On the other hand, she was still very powerful. And she had a small army, too. In fact, she was turning toward her servants even then.

"You and your friends were created to obey me!" she told them. Then she aimed her magic staff at Tridart.

Shaatzzz!

Fiery energy shot out of Nerissa's staff and zapped Tridart right in his icy chest.

"*Urrrrgh!*" he exclaimed.

Irma's jaw dropped. I can't believe it, she thought. The iceman's melting faster than a snowman in a sauna. But why? Why would Nerissa attack her own servant?

"Even if I still possess a copy of the five powers," Nerissa explained to her minions, "I need to recover all of my energy. So I'll take it back from *you!*"

Shaatzzz!

Nerissa's staff sang out again. This time the powerful magic hit Ember. The blast doused her, melting her into a saffron blob.

"Hey! No fair!" Irma cried. "I was supposed

to extinguish her myself!"

But Nerissa wasn't listening to Irma. Or to anyone else. Shagon, the blue-armored giant, had a mask for a face, but his fists were now clenched in anger.

"You can't do that!" he exclaimed. "They've served you well!"

"I know it's unfair," Nerissa replied with an evil little smile. "But all children owe something to their parents. . . . And so it's time for Tridart to break down in tears. And for Ember to return to ashes."

Just as Nerissa had said, Tridart became a puddle of chilly water. And Ember was now a pile of . . . well, *embers*.

"You're cruel!" Shagon proclaimed.

Duh, thought Irma, rolling her eyes. What gave you your first clue?

His fists still clenched, Shagon moved to stand protectively in front of Khor. "Is this what's in store for the two of us?" he asked the sorceress.

"No, Shagon!" Nerissa said with a careless wave. "To generate you, I started out with living material. . . ."

Irma knew that that was true. According to

Caleb, who'd spent time on Mount Thanos, Both Shagon and Khor were living beings who had been transformed into evil beasts, courtesy of Miss Hospitality.

". . . Which is why I want even more from you and Khor," Nerissa told Shagon. "I want your lives!"

Shaatzzz!

Once more, Nerissa had lifted her staff and released a fiery bolt. But this time the magic was brighter and hotter than before. The searing yellow energy enveloped Shagon and Khor together. They screamed out in terrible pain.

"Arrrrrgh!"

Taranee looked alarmed. She turned to the other Guardians. "Shouldn't we do something?"

"Like what?" Irma replied. "Nerissa's doing it all by herself."

The shaggy-haired giant was doubled over in agony. Nerissa's magic was draining him of his powers and his life. And the sorceress just kept on smiling—as if she were enjoying it.

While Irma had to admit that the attack was awful, she also knew that Shagon and Khor would have destroyed the Guardians if Nerissa had commanded them to.

On the other hand, Irma thought, Shagon *does* have one really good trick up his blue armor, *if* he decides to use it.

"I . . . hate . . . you!" Shagon spat.

Nerissa shrugged. "Of course you do, Shagon. You were the paladin of hate. But you were also undisciplined. Well, now you'll make up for it. You'll be the one to give me the extra power I need to—"

"*No-o-o-o-o-o-o-o!*" Shagon cried, suddenly rising up. From behind him, his demon tail whipped around to the front. Like a deadly viper, it struck Nerissa.

"*Aaaaaargh!*" she screamed. The brutal blow was powerful, and Nerissa instantly fell.

Whoomp, there it is! Irma thought. Nerissa forgot the most obvious thing in the world. Shagon grows stronger from hate. And, man, did she get that dude's hate going!

As Nerissa lay fallen, Irma glanced at her fellow Guardians. Will, Hay Lin, Cornelia, and Taranee all looked awesomely ferocious as they stood together, wings fluttering, eyes bright. And Irma knew just what her best friends were thinking. . . .

Bring it on, Nerissa! It's time to end this thing, once and for all. We're W.I.T.C.H., and we are united and strong. The Power of Five is back!